First published 2009 by Cargo Publishing

Copyright © 2009, Andrew Drennan

The moral right of the author has been asserted

Cargo Publishing

www.cargopublishing.com

Printed and bound in England
ISBN 978-0-9563083-0-6

Cover Design by Rachael Gallacher
www.snappymcsnapperson.com

ABOUT THE PUBLISHER

Cargo is a Glasgow based publisher committed to developing new and exciting talent. Cargo is founded on the belief of developing art at grassroots level through new technologies and unconventional promotion.

www.cargopublishing.com

ABOUT THE AUTHOR

Andrew Drennan was born in 1983 and lives in Glasgow. He is the founding editor of the cultural and political blog, The Crowhurst Review which can be found at www.myspace.com/thecrowhurstreview.
Cancer Party is his first novel.

www.myspace.com/cancerparty

CANCER PARTY

ANDREW RAYMOND DRENNAN

To
my mother and father

"'I'm so very sick, you see,' he explained. 'I've tormented and punished myself, without really knowing why…And yesterday, and the day before, and the day before that I've been torturing myself… I'll get better and…stop torturing myself…And what if I never get well? Lord! I'm so tired of it all!…' He kept walking. He longed terribly for some distraction, from that feeling rising up inside him: it was an intolerable loathing for everything around him. All the people he met were repulsive to him: the way they looked at him, the things they said, the way they said them – even their movements filled him with disgust. He had to get away from them all."
- Fyodor Dostoevsky, *Crime and Punishment*

Prologue

'1992. Winter.'

It was a celebration; it was a mourning.

The rain spat down on the frowning tartan umbrellas and ill-fitting trench coats gathered at the graveside. Adam had to strain to release his hand, a tiny bug locked in his father's fist. He knew he should have been concentrating on the words, the ceremony, the celebration the family had tried so hard to make the occasion, but Adam couldn't fathom this turning over of soil on top of a wooden box. All that dressing up just to cry as he had done for the last several days, safe in his room, with his toys, away from prying eyes. He looked out across the plateau of the cemetery grounds, boxed in by some Bronze Age wall no higher than his head. Out past the yellowing fields no trees swayed or blustered: too much wind up there for them to grow. All of Paisley was below; all of its unremarkable skyline of football stadium floodlights and condemned council flats: buried in the middle of a motorway flyover just about visible to Adam, planes took off from Glasgow Airport in seeming haste, the runway behind queued to bursting – each twisting and writhing through the air like a wailing baby tensed and stretched out in your arms – screeching past overhead, loud enough to warrant a pause in Father Dollan's eulogy.

The limo and hearse drivers' heads turned to follow the plane's flight like Wimbledon spectators in slow-motion, leaning on their spades, smoking cigarettes, whose smell would sometimes turn with the wind towards the mourners, the celebrants. A small JCB digger was parked ominously in the background, ready to do the real hard work of filling in the grave. Adam wasn't foolish enough to expect a

1

New Orleans-style parade down the streets with trumpets wailing and white handkerchiefs tossed around in unholy despair, but he hadn't thought it necessary to involve heavy machinery in speeding up the burying of his mother. It saves time, his dad informed him.

"I didn't know we were in such a rush," Adam replied.

They were, however, late for the hotel function room that had been booked; his dad and Aunt Elaine stopping on the way to the cemetery to buy cigarettes at the Jet garage surely hadn't helped. Adam's Uncle Patrick informed him with a genuine sadness that they were now in serious danger of missing the buffet the hotel had laid on.

"In Palestine they mourn the dead for thirty days," Adam explained. In Scotland they mourn until the sausage rolls get cold.

Father Dollan continued his eulogy now that the plane had passed by. He closed his eyes tightly enough for small creases to appear on the upper rim of his cheeks.

"...and we know Lord, that Mairi is now in a better place..."

It had only been a month previous that Adam was skipping school in favour of sitting in church, braving the marble-cold with a few old ladies, his fingers blistered from vigorous, desperate rosaries as his mother's cancer metastasised, spreading greedily from her breast to the rest of her body. He had spent pocket money on candle lighting, trying to tick all the ecclesiastical boxes, as the paintings of the stations of the cross looked down on him, warning him of the perils of dissent. On her deathbed, Mairi wondered how many more candles would have been enough; should she have brought back two litres of holy water from Lourdes and not just the one litre container? Had nuns not made enough dedications in her name, traipsing her around fountains of the Virgin Mary with the other wheelchaired invalids, convalescents and amputees? It was upon seeing the amputees that she realised: God had – rather conveniently – never managed to make entire limbs grow back. God didn't deal with such crass intervention: only the sort of biological chance that might have happened anyway. Even after her hair had fallen out from chemotherapy, she had been reduced to a commode, and her left breast had been scythed from her body, God continued playing a reckless, drunken game of draughts with her red and white blood cells. She would sit on the edge of her bed, waiting for Adam to bring her more tinned mandarins. He would sit at her dressing table and watch her eat in the reflection of the mirror.

Her coffin was lowered down into the ground, the warm blanket around Adam's heart unravelling with the pall bearers' rope. He was desperate to remember it all, like the speedy amnesia of a really great party, and during a bathroom visit you look into the mirror and remind yourself to take it all in, the smells, the tastes, because come the morning you'll be wishing you were back there again. He didn't want it to end.

Adam stepped forward to escape the rain sliding off his Uncle Patrick's umbrella, the drops falling under his collar, working their way down his back before soaking into his white polyester school shirt. The wind suddenly leapt up out from the cover of his dad's stocky frame, whose morning whisky had long soaked into his black suit.

Father Dollan continued: "'For God so loved the world that he gave his one and only Son'-"

"Some father," Adam thought.

"-and as God has shown us his unwavering love and compassion, we will now sing from one of Mairi's favourite hymns, 'Jesus Remember Me'…"

He was actually going to make them sing. No one could say this wasn't a celebration!

And there they were, the Bernadettes, all huddled together under tartan umbrellas, a semi-circle of trench coat hunchbacks filling her grave with tears: the funeral party: the cancer party, singing along at a back-achingly, shoe-shufflingly slow pace, the absence of an organist only dragging out the pain.

Uncle Patrick tried to speed up proceedings, singing ever faster, looking around for everyone else to follow. Which they did. That was fair enough. Everyone's minds were on the waiting buffet. There were sausage rolls getting cold. And drinks getting warm.

Chapter One

'1997. Winter.'

The bath had made a decent bed for the night, the cold enamel slowly warming against Adam's skin, his eyes yet to start burning from another sleepless night – that would come later in the daylight. He splashed some water on his face, avoiding the unwelcome scrutiny of the shaving light above the mirror, highlighting the disaster of his eyes. With everyone he had spoken to just a few hours before, their eyes inevitably wandered from his, sensing behind those stray, vacant pupils hidden under his thin sweeping fringe of hair, that he was on some sort of medication.

It had started as a typically decadent birthday party for some GOMA Kid called Deek, whose gender Adam never really learned, even upon meeting them, and even after Deek had stuck his or her tongue down his throat in thanks for supplying the party with copious amounts of Xanax and Lustral. Adam never trusted favours from his buyers, and certainly not unspecific-gender ones. At least his pills managed to keep the swimming-in-fountains and television-tossing antics of the GOMA Kids at bay for one more night. Feather boas were thrown with slightly more restraint, and lines of powder were hoovered up less copiously than usual.

Adam crept out the bathroom, remembering the bottle of Totov vodka he had taken in as his sleeping partner, the door creaking open loudly, prompting calls of 'shut the fuck up' from the bodies littering the long, cold hallway in front of him – a graveyard of beer cans, wine and cider bottles. The party victims lay passed out in rooms whose function was impossible to say. Furniture had been turned over in bedrooms and studies: not that mattered a great deal. Regular was the sight in the morning after a GOMA Kids' party of teenagers carving out cheques on cider-drenched carpets; amounts to cover the damage they had caused to whoever had been reckless enough to invite them round. The cheques always had their father's names next to their own: a private slush fund of excess linked to trust fund accounts meant for university. It was a long shot that some of them would even make it as far as the next summer, if the parties of the last three months were anything to go by.

In one such destroyed room Adam found three skeletal thin teenagers on a what looked like a bed – a boy and two girls, all bones and smudged makeup. One of the girls stirred from his movement at the door, rolling over on to her side. The inside of her arm had the word 'STOIC' freshly cut into her pale white skin, the blood now soft and translucent like a watercolour painting left in the summer rain. A razorblade and an empty bottle of Aftershock lay on the floor next to the bed, now a dead bee that had delivered its sting.

Behind Adam, his cousin Edward's footsteps were squeaking up the staircase. "What's wrong?" he enquired. He was wearing a pair of two-tone blue Y-fronts, a bowler hat and drinking from the same bottle of J&B whisky Adam had left him with.

"I thought maybe they were dead," Adam said, his voice slender and weak, as if his vocal chords were wrung out like a dispassionate housewife strangling a kitchen towel.

Edward squinted into the darkness of the room, the rank potpourri of ashtrays scattered around the floor overwhelming the senses. He noticed Fiona lying on the bed, her arm turned over in the

6

growing light from the door. "Stoic, eh?" Edward said brusquely, taking a long swig from his bottle before getting dressed.

The scrawny little bird on the bed awoke now, a lost puppy of acceptance in her voice. "You're leaving."

He bent down and tied his shoe laces with brisk, forceful pumps. "There's a horse I need to go bet on," he sighed, without looking at her. He went down the stairs.

Adam stood for a second before offering, "What can I say, Fi? Your arm has the answer…" With Totov in hand he followed Edward downstairs, passing a boy called Bug making his way towards Fiona's room.

His eyes were still wide from Ecstasy, his mouth chomping and stretched out to the sides, his trembling fingers doing up his school tie, though he would never make it to the school grounds. He would just be hanging out on the steps of the Gallery of Modern Art with all the others. They never went in to the exhibitions. They just sat on the steps, consoling each other with…with...

Bug looked around the room – the spilt bottle of wine, the tear-soaked sheets, the sudden glint in her eye. Fiona pulled the covers down and he took his tie back off.

The cold air gusted against Adam's face as Eddie slammed the front door shut behind them. Pigeons burst out in all directions from behind the trees across the street, as if choreographed by some National Theatre director, sending the last of the brown leaves to the ground. Rich old ladies were already up walking their manicured dogs, oblivious to the horrors in the plush townhouse the two boys had just left.

Edward held onto the tip of his bowler hat, a steady drizzle falling so slowly Adam could follow single drops falling in the orange glow of the streetlights. He swallowed two Percocet dry and almost gagged on them. "Cold even for October," he said looking up at the black, pre-dawn sky. "First day of winter today."

Edward wandered aimlessly into the path of a wheelie bin, making no attempt to stop it falling over, spraying the pavement with the empty packets of microwaveable meals and home pregnancy tests. Still straddling the bin, he snarled, "It's always fucking freezing around here. No wonder you're all so thoroughly ugly. It's not your fault, I s'pose. I bet you like it, don't you. All of this fucking Larkin misery."

"It's more Dickens, actually. *This* helps, though." Adam took a swig. "You're still going home today, aren't you?"

Edward didn't answer.

"I thought you might have shagged enough GOMA Kids to have gotten it out your system by now. I'm sure your fellow fee-paying school friends will be most impressed."

He tutted. "Not much impresses them. Most of them will be in southern France right now, touring vineyards with their insufferable parents, and shagging bakers' daughters behind bistros at night. What do I get? This. This *shit*."

"You should just get yourself straightened out. Hutchie starts back next week and it's just as well you're leaving today—"

"You know, I really wish you'd speak up, I can never understand you," he pouted and took another drink, falling back against a wall

8

graffitied with the tag: 'The Eton Boys'.

Adam sat on the kerb of the pavement, burying his head between his knees, desperately trying to remain conspicuous – a difficulty at his awkward six foot height, but he remained committed to the task, allowing his weight to fall to that of any dedicated alcoholic.

Eddie minced gingerly around the empty bus stop, too proud to say he was feeling unwell, but it was there in his face: gaunt, pale white, and dark shadow rings under his eyes from several almost sleepless nights with Adam. Not entirely what his Uncle Patrick and Aunt Elaine had had in mind when they shipped Edward off into his care for the last dregs of autumn.

The Glasgow-Paisley bus came speeding towards the two, blasting its horn for Adam to get off the road edge.

"Alright, asshole," he grumbled, just escaping the splash of gutter water.

Edward barged in front, saying, "I'll handle this." Then he said to the turbaned driver, pointing to himself, "I…am…*Scot…tish.*"

The driver said, unmoved, "You don't sound it, pal."

"Hey!" he said, happily surprised, "he speaks English. Well done, you. I mean, I'm all in favour of you Turks joining the EU."

Adam pushed Edward aside and said to the driver, "Ignore him," and handed him their student passes for discounted travel.

Edward stood in the middle of the aisle and announced to the sleepy commuters - after a mouthful of J&B - "Here's a joke for all you peasants! There's this totally empty desert island. Just sand, no trees, nothing. Then a Paki, a Frenchman, and an Irishman get shipwrecked…"

Adam couldn't muster the energy to intervene; his mere association with Edward was enough to merit everyone's disdain. "I'm sorry about this…" he mumbled as Eddie finished the joke:

"…and the Paki says, that's alright for you Murphy, but I've got nowhere to open my corner shop. Haha!"

"OK then?" Adam asked the driver again, siphoning coins out of his pocket onto the metal tray. The driver had a tiny photo of himself on his badge that made him look like an imminent suicide. Below it read, 'Teddy – I'm here to help'.

Eddie snatched the tickets from the machine and tossed them in the air. "What's with you fucking people? No sense of humour…come on Adam, let's sit at the back and have a drink." He jabbed his finger on the shoulders of some of the passengers, barking, "Good morning, slaves!" at them, followed by more mad cackling. No one seemed to notice much, just keeping their dead eyes focussed out of the window.

Eddie opened a window at the back of the bus so he could smoke a cigarette - although the bus was cold enough to see your breath, the only real sign of life on the bus.

"Look at this dump," Eddie slurred, the cigarette in his mouth the wrong way round, eyeing the passing decaying streets. "My grandfather died in a war for this place."

"You told me your grandfather shot himself because he was going on trial for cowardice."

"That's still dying in a war, Adam."

The bus stopped at traffic lights beside the newsagent the GOMA Kids had tried to burn down a few months earlier when the proprietor refused to sell them booze. A man Adam faintly recognised idled past, smoking a rollup cigarette. He, too, looked like he had suffered some indignities the night before. He was dwarfed by a gigantic advertising hoarding behind him, a New Labour election campaign poster with Tony Blair's face beaming a few metres wide, with their catchphrase below: 'Because Britain deserves better.'

Edward pointed in the man's direction. "Hey...isn't that your dad?"

Adam replied after one fast, sharp look. "No."

"How is the old man these days? We should go down the pub and meet him. After all that's where he's most likely to be on a Monday morning, isn't it?"

"Don't be stupid. He won't be in the pub till at least eleven. He'll be on his way to sign on."

"That might have been him, then. He might-"

"Just leave it, Eddie."

Crossing the King George Bridge out of Glasgow – the edges of buildings clear and defined against the frosty air - the evil, ever-shifting cumulus faces in the sky appeared all too human to him.

Presently Adam and Edward fell off the bus, one tripping into the other. Adam feebly offered the driver a 'peace' sign as he pulled away.

"What now?" Edward asked.

Adam pointed towards Barshaw Park across the road. "We go get more drunk in there. It'll be nice and quiet."

"There's not much booze left."

"Too early to buy more."

They both considered being sick after dashing through the heavy traffic to get to the park, but neither were ready to capitulate yet.

"Want to race?" Edward asked.

"I've got more left than you."

But before Adam could argue further, Edward counted off, "One, two, three, GO!"

They clasped their lips around their bottles and let their faces turn up to the sky.

A few hours later they were woken by a group of sun bed sun-tanned mothers the size of cars, discussing what television they had been watching that morning. It was now lunchtime.

They all had the same Burberry design prams, each of them puffing away rabidly on cigarettes, suckling on the tarry goodness. The smoke hung in front of their faces in dense clouds - every pore seeping poison. A thin layer of snow had since covered Adam and Edward's bodies. Edward was first to stir.

He brushed the snow off. "Christ! I could have frozen to death. Adam, you fucking reprobate, waken up immediately." The snow had done little to rid them of their stupor and the sudden movement proved fatal for Edward. "Don't just sit there, Adam, get me a bucket."

He leant over the bench and retched over what would have been a flower bed in summertime.

Adam looked over his shoulder with a sigh. "You have to eat something before you can throw up, Eddie."

One thing was for sure: Winter had arrived; the days would only get darker from now on, and there was nowhere to hide.

"I know what we need to do, Eddie."

"What?"

"Get out of this fucking park."

The rest of the afternoon had a desperate affair, trying to warm themselves up with whisky and blankets. Adam was first to succumb to sleep on his sofa, woken only by the clatter of the front door. Edward was gone, along with three bottles of Adam's most expensive wines (which still didn't break the £20 mark). He now sat on the edge of his bed, a light box beaming from his bedside table, the only thing that stemmed his Seasonal Affective Disorder, a state brought on by the shortened winter days. After all, these were dark times. Adam was always surprised at how many people it affected; all these people looking for light. But he was a man…no, that's not right, he was a *product* of his times.

The sickness of the morning finally purged itself from his body in sweat and vomit (if the human body was such a miracle of design, then where were the clean, efficient, scent-free excretions? Why did everything have to cause so much mess?). The assortment of pills by his bed were swallowed by rote, by now an elaborate equation that *just made sense*, like a familiar phone number: two Percocet to increase the seratonin levels in his brain, followed by a Seroxat to offset the drowsiness in the morning because of the Percocet; then one Lustral in case the Seroxat left him nauseous during the night - and finally one Paxil to help with sleep.

The last piece of the ritual was turning the picture of his mother around and kissed it goodnight; then he turned it back so it faced the wall again, like always.

13

Chapter Two

'Cat'

It was already getting dark on Cat's street, each an extraordinary mansion of unlit rooms, vacant dwellings, of lives constantly lived somewhere else, always travelling: someone get them a destination!

Then Cat's house came, lights on in every room, curtains thoughtlessly blowing out open windows. Concerns out there in the 'burbs were two holidays abroad a year; reading allegorical books written by tanned Latin Americans about the nature of 'being'; finding schools without a 'bad element' (that meant Adam).

An audience of the usual suspects watched his approach from the imperiously high lounge window, whisky and wine glasses in hand, ready to see what he would be supplying the party with.

"Adam, where have you been?" Cat cried hyperactively, running down the front stairs.

"You don't want to—"

"Ohmygod I think I had a nervous breakdown last night!" she exclaimed, grabbing hold of him, then desperately fanned her face with her hands. "It was the weirdest thing. It was like everything was fine and then I thought…ohmygod what if I die to*day*?" She threw her hands up in the air and waited for a response.

"Em…yeah I guess. But you didn't eh?"

"I'm OK now," she added.

"I didn't ask," he mumbled to himself.

"What?"

"I said I'm not sure a nervous breakdown lasts one night, Cat."

Her body was a rain-smeared window to a darker place.

15

Following the publicity of her internet blog, Cat had become a minor hit with her tales of sex with strange men (most when she was still a minor). A major London magazine was now commissioning her own column, complete with a cover page of her crying – provided she started to include tales of drug-taking and self-harm, despite the fact that Cat did neither. 'Blood makes good copy these days,' they told her. 'After Richey Edwards from the Manic Street Preachers disappeared, there's been a major gap in the self-harm market.' So now she had become a self-harming drug addict.

There she stood slumped in the doorway, sporting a barrage of bandages down her arm, the magazine's adverts for how depressed she was, like a catatonic Formula One driver. She was wearing a short black frilly skirt with pink polka dot tights accentuating her keen, desperate thighs. Her breasts bubbled out and over her vest top like smack melting in a spoon. She showed off fresh red gashes on her arms; on her left arm the scars were deeper (she was right handed) and fresh, uncovered. Bleeding for money, for love.

"Been working tonight, Cat?" Adam asked, looking worriedly at the ever-increasing depth of the cuts from what she had started off with a few months ago. The blood was still running, in fact.

The magazine's subsidised depression was once no more than a spilled drink, an appliance left on overnight. Now her grief looked akin to an earthquake survivor who had lost all their family; it was turning into terminal illness-grief. House repossession.

"The magazine wants me to kill myself next month," she said blankly. She opened a small prescription bottle and downed a number of white pills. "Well, not really. Just pretend. They'll bring back my column after Christmas. No one ever buys more than two issues anyway."

Lady Lazarus.

"So, who's here?" Adam asked. "What does everyone want?"

She slipped the bottle down into the nest of her cleavage, like a bird warming her eggs. "The usual. But Nicholas won't be here, he's down the police station."

"What? What for?"

"He shaved his head and tried to check himself into hospital. Cherry said they ran some tests and said he was pretending he had cancer."

Everyone has got cancer.

Nicola appeared in the window, holding an empty prescription bottle. She was mouthing: "Got any more?"

"You look like shit," Cat assured me. "Is that a Joy Division T-shirt? I love how their singer tries to sound *really* miserable."

"Well, he *did* end up hanging himself—"

"Hanging yourself? Slash your wrists for fuck's sake – now *that's* fucking hardcore. None of this hanging yourself bollocks."

Only Cat could embrace the public spectacle of self destruction via *razorus bladus*. Slashing had become the way forward for suicide in the soundbite generation. What do you do when killing yourself isn't good enough?

"Let's go inside," he said, readying his supplies of powders and pills in his coat pocket.

"Did you bring any drink? It's OK if you didn't, dad left loads in the garage, the magazine sent me loads of books and films to name-drop in my next column, most of them are rubbish, or so I've been told anyway, I just don't have the time. Everyone's next door, take off your jacket, oh you don't have one, aren't you cold…"

Trying to stop her talking was like leaping onto an escalator travelling in the opposite direction to yourself. "Stop, stop! What's with you?"

She laughed. "Oh, it's just the coke, makes me run my mouth off. Oh!" She clapped her hands. "The magazine sent me the book for that character, Miss Tralala, my column's named after. The Harry Selby Jnr one."

"You mean Hubert."

She wasn't listening. "Totally. He's, like, this really cool writer. Apparently. It's tres cool, huh?"

Adam sighed. "So the magazine chose the name of your column?"

"Yeah," she laughed.

He edged his way inside. Nicola was standing by the study room door, anxious to be first in line for whatever Adam had to offer. People buzzed around her, shouting for drinks (vodka straight!), song requests (Portishead!), lost shoes (black Converse!), extra-safe condoms (don't bother, just make sure you pull out!).

Everyone drinking, yelling, screaming, running, crying, laughing, pissing, punching, kicking, fucking – but always drinking.

Cat was like everyone else, and typically Scottish: fatherless. She never saw him and when she did he didn't care because he was a lawyer and his whole profession was about lying and deceit; and by the look of her house Adam could tell he must have been pretty good

18

at it. Her mum never did anything, but she always seemed to require lots of rest, heavily sedated in country health retreats, and spas – as long as they had decent mini bars. Yes, that would help mother get her strength back… When they were ten, Cat and Adam used to play doctors and nurses with her as she lay passed out on the bed with a bottle of Lithium.

Presently Cat was talking to Cherry, who sat on the floor, nodding occasional "yeah yeah yeahs", setting up lines of coke on a handheld mirror. The proceeds from Cat's first pay cheque from the magazine. London paid well.

Dick's arm lassoed Adam into the lounge which was in near darkness. Two-fat-lovers-seeing-each-other-naked-for-the-first-time darkness, lit only by a dull lamp on the floor in the corner of the room. Dick was rolling a joint on top of that week's NME (yet another cover of Oasis draped in Union Jack, which had now become – unknown to the band – 'ironic''), of which there were several copies scattered around the room, all turned to the letters page.

On the oak coffee table lay Adam's, now tattered, copy of 'Last Exit to Brooklyn', currently being used as a coaster.

Dick threw his bag of weed down and screamed to the room across the hall, "TOM! Will you please put on SOMETHING FUCKING MELLOW!"

"There's a pile of Icelandic post rock CDs in my bag, go get them," said Tom casually who was sitting right at Dick's feet. He was wearing a T-shirt that said '(Post) Punk is Dead'. If Tom had been in the Garden of Eden when it all kicked off, he would still have found something to be 'post…' about. Post Creation Sucks. Dick was

19

wearing the exact same clothes as the skinny rock star on the magazine cover.

"What is with this tragic music situation, Adam? 'Sup man! You got some shit for me?" Dick held out his hand for Adam to shake like hip hoppers, but he got his hands all muddled up. The reaction round the room was like he had tried to shoot a porno in Islamabad city square.

Dick sniggered, "*Whatever* dude…you got my gear?"

"Sure." Adam handed him a small baggy of Percocet and some Seroxat. All the stuff he sold was his own prescription, that, or stolen from the parents of his friends: 100% profit. Apparently getting out of your head wasn't just a youthful endeavour.

Next to Dick was Harry, whose head was buried in a literary magazine he had imported from America called Zoon. Harry asked, "Hey Adam, have you read the new Sharman Shapiro Ng? You *have* to read it. I mean, I've only read the reviews, but all the right ones love it!"

"I don't know, I don't have much money for books right now."

He grabbed Adam's arm. "But he's the new voice of nihilistic youth in America."

"But I don't care about America."

"You've got to care about America! Everyone else does."

Adam stared back.

Harry started to cry. "It's…it's critically acclaimed!" he pleaded, trying to hold back sobs.

Tom changed the CD. "Check this out, Dick."

For the next two minutes the room was filled with what sounded like a car engine struggling to catch, accompanied by drum and bass throng. The three boys sat in a tidy row smoking the joint and nodding their heads in unison to a rabid, incoherent beat.

"This DJ is a *fucking* genius," Tom said.

"Who is he?" asked Harry.

"He doesn't like...have a *name*. It's like, you know that noise a lighter makes when you flick it? It's that. Kind of like Sharman Shapiro *Ng* actually," Tom smiled, impressed at his own knowledge.

"How do you ask for that in a shop?" Adam asked.

The three boys stared at him and tutted one after the other. "That's not the *point*, Adam."

"That's not the point, Adam."

"Yeah, that's not the point, Adam."

Tom added, "He's one of the leading figures in Belgian thrash-hardcore-industrial-disco right now!"

Dick nodded, "That's a tough scene to crack, you know."

Harry threw a coaster at Adam. "Ask me how my band is going."

"How is your band going, Harry?"

They were called 'Fucking Miss Daisy'.

He jumped to his feet, frantically lighting a cigarette as if incapable of discussing the band without one. "It's going fucking great. Now this whole Britpop thing is dying, and everyone's over that whole 'things can only get better' shite, we've been talking to this guy in New York about you know, laying down a few tracks. I don't know if we can be bothered though. New York's so fucking...so..."

"I know, man..." nodded Dick.

"I know, man…" nodded Tom.

Adam escaped, stepping over the pairs of black and white Converse shoes littering the hall, and went into the lounge. Cat was holding her new copy of 'The Bell Jar', shaking it around whilst talking at length about the similarities between herself and Sylvia Plath's life. The magazine encouraged it.

"…I mean I've never had really black depression *per se*…"

The room was captivated and everyone nodded along vacantly, like her very own little puppet show, as if they all had strings attached underneath their chins, so whenever someone spoke or offered an opinion, it would blithely move up and down to avoid embarrassing the host.

"…I did try to put my head in the oven when I was six but it wasn't on…"

She placed 'The Bell Jar' next to two further copies of it on the shelf, none of the spines cracked.

"…and it was only one of those plastic Fisher Price ones…"

Nicola stood at the bar downing shots, those reckless, ragged eyes of hers piercing out across the room towards Cat.

"…but I'm sure once I find my Ted Hughes…"

Cherry shouted for Adam from the hall, crouched over some lines laid out on a mirror, a nicotine-stained finger running through her pink dyed hair. "Adam there's some…guy here for you."

At the front door stood Donald. He wasn't invited - he never was.

"Hey, Adam!" he chirped.

He quickly hid the bottle of pills he was holding in his trousers.

22

"Donald, I'm not carrying tonight."

Donald had already firmly established himself on benefits since leaving school, which caused problems for him when I came to scoring. His mum and dad were concerned about Donald when he started hanging around with kids who wore AC/DC t-shirts all the time and were inclined to shoot stray dogs with air rifles. Although he was dropped as a baby, the truth was 80's hair metal had destroyed his brain far worse than a lack of healthy social interaction.

"You getting really *fucking* wasted tonight then?" he said.

"No...Probably...I don't know..."

"Well are—"

"Look, I've got to go see someone next door Donald, so what's up?"

He flopped his hair back up and stood to the side, allowing Adam to see to the end of the driveway, a gaggle of teenagers waited, hanging through the entrance gate. They were the clingers-on of the GOMA Kids, those without enough money to behave like one, like the real GOMA Kids sitting inside with Adam.

"Yeah man, I'm here to see Cat."

"Cat? Are you sure? What are all of them doing here? You know how the others feel about..."

"Yeah man, I know. Cat's kind of taking a wee trip with us in a few days."

"Cat doesn't take acid, Donald."

"Oh no, man, not like that. An actual trip."

Adam sighed, "Well, you better come in and speak to her then."

Donald signalled to the others he'd be back in five minutes.

23

Cat appeared, lipstick smudged since Adam last saw her. "Donald."

"You told me to come talk about...the *thing*. The Fur King thing."

"You still working there, Donald?" Adam asked.

"I meant..." Cat started, looked towards the lounge, "during the day," and ushered him to the upstairs landing.

Adam went to the kitchen, remembering an unattended bottle of Jack Daniels someone left out. He knew you had to be ruthless when you're a drinker. Taking no prisoners. Not yours? There was no reasoning with Adam's bloodstream. It simply didn't work, especially when it had had five units an hour since lunchtime swilling through it. He filled his glass to the top, downing it straight, his throat burning, screaming for mercy. Cat and Donald's voices approached the kitchen door, so Adam grabbed the bottle and his behind the fridge. Cat showed Donald out the back door, saying, "Don't worry, I'll get him to come," and then sauntered back to the lounge.

Adam stepped out from the shadows and refilled his glass with a more reasonably sized measure, before rejoining the others.

Lucy shushed the others, saying, "Hey, Adam, did you actually bring any booze of your own this time?"

Tom, Dick and Harry didn't try hard to stop their laughter spluttering through their hands. Lucy smiled, pleased with herself.

"If you're all taken care of, then I can just go."

Cat remonstrated with Dick for putting his feet up on the sofa. "Hey, that's an antique. My dad says it's been distressed. It's very expensive. Very expensive." She took Adam's arm and led him to the drinks cabinet. "I've just got the best scoop for the magazine. Donald and his lot, the bunch outside, they're having a party at Donald's work."

"What? The Fur King?"

"That's right. Donald asked if you could bring along some toys."

"What does he want to play with?"

"Some of those nice energetic pink ones. And the yellow ones."

"Sure."

"We'll meet at the Fur King on Friday."

"Why can't I just meet you or Donald in town before?"

"Look, Donald has this new crowd he's running with, he wants them to see all the people he knows." She held her hand against her chest and grimaced. "Oh fuck…I'm not having a heat attack, am I?"

Adam stared back. "You're not having a heart attack."

"Good." She swigged heavily from a bottle of vodka with a pill or two. "Party Time. That's what the magazine wants me to call the piece."

"Of course," Adam said deadpan.

Cat danced into the middle of the room. "Hey, do any of you have a cigarette - I mean, I don't really smoke but I'd like to hold one for a while?"

"Hey, what's that you're taking?" asked Harry.

"Percocet. Adam's got a good supply."

"Yeah, I'm sure my mum used to take those."

Adam leaned over the flap of the drinks cabinet, rolling a joint on the leather surface.

Arthur was reading a poem he had been writing in front of the fireplace that night. He raised his glass high in the air and announced, "Remember this…" allowing a dramatic pause, "scream at the sky, wail at the empty streets…"

While the others had formed a circle around Arthur's feet (how like children sharing their toys), Nicola joined Adam, standing back at the drinks cabinet. She hadn't noticed how impenetrably dark the room was until Adam flicked the lighter to soften the hash, the flame creeping up towards his face. Only a few tea candles were lit on the coffee table, and the fireplace was glowing coolly now, lighting the room in a purgatorial hue, ill defining the features of their young faces. They could have been the ravaged bodies of old men and women by the way they moved.

Arthur's voice built to a shout for the final line, "Let us rejoice in the death of the light."

Spontaneous applause and whooping broke out, leading Arthur to give a gentle bow to his audience. "Come on," he said, urging the others to follow him to the study, across the vast hallway, "Let's raid the library."

Cat added, "Yeah, I left a mean brandy in there."

Nicola passed the joint to Adam, watching rain begin to skiffle through the open window. She put 'Moon Dreams' by Miles Davis on the record player, taking a seat on the window ledge beside a large globe on an oak stand as large as a child. She was running her bare foot across it, turning the world over and over as fast as she chose.

"He's," Adam cleared his throat, "a *poet*."

Nicola's eyes rolled back and forth like overhead lights on a night-time motorway. "He's got a Dylan Thomas haircut."

The breeze from the window blew the scent of her perfume towards him, all the decay of tobacco in the room extinguishing. The others were in the study, taking poppers on the floor, listening to Arthur recite 'Howl' from memory.

As Adam approached, his face appeared indistinct and rearranged like a weeping Picasso portrait in the reflection of Nicola's glitter dress. "It's not going to stop anytime soon. The rain, I mean."

Nicola closed the curtains over the image she had drawn in the condensation. "I haven't seen you since Deek's birthday last week."

"That's right. Do you know him well? Did he have a good time?"

"He? Deek's a girl."

Adam smiled to himself.

"What's so funny?"

"Nothing."

Her heart was still racing from an E taken hours before in her bedroom, watching her council estate speed by through a stubborn dusk: the boy racers had travelled at hyper-speeds, the rear lights stretching out in vapour trails past Nicola's bedroom; fights outside the park seemed to be over in seconds; old men shuffling along with sticks now sprinted past in tiny steps. To Nicola, it was the perfect drug, to speed up time, to get to the end of the day quicker.

Cherry wandered in, her footsteps crisscrossing in some exaggerated supermodel's strut. She was giggling behind her hand which was still lightly salted with white powder around the fingertips. "Hey you two – I was sitting there listening to Arthur, and I couldn't

27

stop laughing because I had nothing to say. Nothing!"

"It'll wear off, Cherry," Adam said. "You should drink a little something."

She took a bottle, seemingly at random, from the open drinks cabinet, then downed in a row the remainders of whatever glasses were still sitting on the lounge table. There was hardly an unavailable surface that didn't have an empty glass standing on it. CDs littered the carpet, discarded with as much haste and vigour as they were chosen.

Cherry paused in the doorway, the light of the chandelier above the sweeping hall staircase flooding her left side; she looked as she truly was: still just a girl, skinny, and sunken eyes that constantly scowled 'why are you looking at me?'. Her hair was already turning to string thanks to its relentless dyeing and twisting; the structure of her face allowed Adam – even at her tender age – to be imagined as an old woman; it would only take a few wrinkles and the slightest greying in hair colour to see it, the frailty of a girl holding a bottle that didn't contain summery colours. They were always the murky browns of rums and whiskies, or the disarming clarity of vodka. "Tell me, Adam," she said, "are you going to Commit Suicide?"

The question didn't seem to surprise him. "I very much doubt it. The wrist thing would be too sore, hanging makes your eyes bulge out like a cartoon character being strangled, jumping off a building or a bridge draws it out too long, and overdosing could leave you in a coma for the rest of your life, and no one round here has a gun. So I think my best chance is an accidental overdose."

"No, no, I meant the Halloween club night at the Pillbox - it's called 'Commit Suicide'. The idea is to dress up as a method of suicide. I think I'm going to go as an abortion."

Nicola gave the globe another roll with her foot, taking a drink every third revolution. "I don't think that counts as suicide. Technically that's just death."

"Hmm. Well, I would have aborted myself if I was conscious. So technically…"

Adam knocked back a whisky and smirked. "As long as the intent was there, that's what counts."

Suddenly Harry appeared in the doorway. "How gut-wrenching."

"How truly sad-making," Tom added behind him.

"Arthur's going to try 'The Wasteland' next if you want to come back through." He went up on tiptoes to look at Adam. "I think we're all taken care of here, now, Adam. Thanks and all…but there must be more GOMA Kids out there that could do with your supplies right now?"

Cherry and Tom and Harry returned to the study, laughing with each other, gliding across the marble like they were on ice skates.

Nicola watched the globe slowly come to a stall, resting her toe on Scotland. "Don't we look small from up here," she said. "You know the worst thing I could say is about myself is that I don't care I'm not unique, that I'm not special or remarkable. It makes sense that seeing as the world is so huge…there must be some people on here that are forgotten about. And they just keep getting spun around by some drunk above them."

"That *is* sad-making."

She paused, letting her smile just hang there, hoping it would get the truth out of him. "Why do you come here? It's not for the money, hardly anyone pays you."

"I do alright."

"You could do better elsewhere."

"That's why I've had to get a job. By the looks of my first student loan, I'm not going to cut it otherwise."

"Yeah, it's hard keeping up, isn't it."

Adam's hand trembled in his pocket as he worked out whether or not to try and pull her closer to kiss her. There is a certain radar of proximity that has to be broken before it seems so inevitable that the pair have no real option left other than to kiss.

Adam said, "I heard once that the definition of madness is repeating the same behaviour over and over again and expecting different results."

Nicola put the needle back to the start of 'Moon Dreams' again, and lit a cigarette with slow deliberate movements. "We must be mad as hatters, then."

They shared an E and watched the rain falling down on the exquisite garden outside, the spray from the fountain shooting up into the white lights underneath the water surface, like it was coming alive, the water reversing back upwards into clouds again, the angelic sculpture looming over it, her eyes alive and alive.

The bright headlights of a car suddenly filled the lounge and Nicola and Adam's scared bodies. Cries of "what the fuck?" interrupted the reading next door.

Nicola asked, "What should we do if it's Cat's dad?"

"He won't be back home until Christmas."

"Her mum?"

"I think Cherry said Stobo Castle spa."

The driver – in silhouette - flashed the headlights at the house.

"I think they're flashing at you," Adam said.

"Oh Christ, is that the time already…" She stood up, stumbling a few paces to the side as she pieced her clothes together from the stack of scarves and hats and gloves dumped on the floor next to Cat's bulging bookcases. She turned in the doorway, and said with tedious inevitability in her voice, "I'll probably see you at the next Fucking Miss Daisy gig, I suppose."

"I suppose," Adam replied, sounding equally bored.

As she closed the door over, a gust of wind blew the curtains back, the car headlights showing what Nicola had been drawing in the condensation in the window: a heart with an arrow through it. Shot to pieces.

Adam put the needle back to the opening of 'Moon Dreams', pouring himself another drink as the car reversed out the driveway. Arthur could be heard in the background, reciting away at 'The Wasteland'. Adam give the globe as hard a spin as he could manage. "Mad as hatters," he said to himself.

Chapter Three

'Pablo the Hero'

Around three that morning, Adam was woken by the sound of dogs barking and a woman screaming. He tumbled off his sofa, still degenerately drunk, knocking over the beer bottles on the floor as he stumbled to the window. A drunken girl was caught up in a fight with some tracksuit types. Her eyes were heavily panda'd, tears shed for some footballer, no doubt. How she missed his taught muscles and perfect hair. She was trying to run as fast as she could, but her tight white miniskirt clung to her behind like a body-size condom, restricting her run to a pusillanimous trot, her heels kicking back so high she tripped every few steps – boobs bouncing, barely contained in her halter-neck top, as the fight spread across the whole street. Traffic (taxis and boy racers) had stopped on either side of them, but they didn't bother blowing their horns. They knew they were liable to get a brick put through their windscreens. They all did u-turns and drove away, leaving the street free for the fight.

They threw anything and everything they could: litter bins, the bread crates outside the corner shop; some even tore the phone box door off its hinges, although it was so heavy they could only throw it a few feet. Adam sat perched on his window sill, calmly smoking a cigarette.

The police were smart, and didn't start their sirens until it was too late for them to scatter. They threw the ones that were too slow to get away into the back of the police van to take them home. It wasn't worth anyone's effort to arrest them, book them and clog the cells up; there were too many other booze hounds and needle magnets in

33

Paisley that needed them.

Pre-empting a miserable hangover, Adam fixed himself some water from the kitchen tap, staring out the window to the warehouse roof opposite where a small group of pigeons had flown down and settled. They had made a nest in the corner of the guttering and snuggled together. All together as a family. The water gushed over the top of the glass as he continued to stare.

The morning came wrapped in a freezing cold fog. The visibility so dense the sun had lost all its brightness; Adam had never realised just how perfectly circular the sun was until then. Rather than scoring or helping others score, he had business to attend to: it was his first day at the oversize DIY store, Fix It, located in the River Dale retail park in Glasgow. This was not to be confused with the River *Oak* retail park, just outside Paisley, although they are both owned by the same company – soon there would be 'River' franchises all over Scotland. A local MP remarked, *Maybe if they open up enough we'll all drown.*

The bus was filled with sad reveries of the future: the self-consciously bald businessman, crushed up against the window, terrified of bodily contact with the woman next to him. How he dreamt of the freedom of a car. Behind him, a student frantically cramming; an old woman with a wig she didn't think anyone else noticed, and so wandered the aisles of Marks and Spencer's with grace, unafraid to ask for assistance from the young man and his discerning eye; silent junkies at the back, nothing to say until the score; and at the front, a single mother, greasy blonde hair hauled back with a multipurpose band, the sleeves of her black sweater recklessly rolled up, the words 'Hugo Boss' peeling off, crudely printed on the cheap fabric. Her two little children were adorned with similar knock-off attire, ready to face the world with fake, misleading clothes: to think that they would 'make it' with such clear disparities of the authentic! No: Scotland demanded a more genuine article now, from their clothes, to their television chat shows, to their Swedish furniture, to their Prime Minister.

The Barrowlands' tyrannical neon sign buzzed insistently above the market place. Crowds gathered in the back alleys buying pirate computer software, dump bins filled with professionally knocked off underwear from Marks and Spencer's. The pavements a matinee of piss theatre, spilled booze fermenting in the afternoon sun with the daytime drunks. One of them sat cross legged on the pavement, a can of Skol super-lager in his hand, asking for change outside an off license that appeared to be simply called 'booze', all in - surely unnecessary - lower case lettering.

"Awright pal, howsit goin' guvnor..." he cheered the pedestrians and tourists as they walked past. He had a street drinker's tan - a combination of dirt, tar, and sunshine. A cut-up Burger King coffee cup lay by his feet, pushed deep into the slipstream of the busy pavement – no sign, no statement of beneficiaries, nothing of being 'hungry and homeless' - not even an income-sapping mangy mutt by his side - yet people were giving him money based solely on a cup on the ground. One of his pungent chums shuffled past him, calling him 'Pablo'. Ah yes: Pablo. That *had* to be his name. He would instil a sense of achievement in all the good Scottish people that saw him. What a fine example of how Scotland was coming up. Anyone could make it with nothing but a paper cup and a smile. Pablo. He was their Hero.

River Dale was set on the banks of the River Clyde, the entrance dominated by a white arch way that stretched from one side of the street to the other, like the giant swords beckoning the entrance to Baghdad. This was the great New Country, all twisted metal and abstract statues coiled on the ground like dog faeces. On a four-lane roundabout under the archway, the Scottish flag flapped victoriously on a high white pole: the watchman observing the sea of people dreaming of improvement. And what better place to practice Scotland's new found sense of The Future than Fix It. Now houses could be a Mecca of matching fabrics, a Paradise of Picasso prints – the Scots were chasing after self-improvement as if stuck on a treadmill, the speed always building and the finishing line was still on a horizon never coming.

There were no horizons in the veritable aircraft hangar that was Fix It, only metal corrugated walls. Bright red signs were everywhere, revealing only more signs telling you where to find more signs. Arrows pointed in all directions, each clawing for the attention of the unconscious. Shoppers rolled about elaborately-shaped trolleys, each like a mini-foreman, confidently browsing, faces grim with intent, heads full of lists.

The tannoy announced, "A member of Paint to the tills please, *urgent* assistance required." They had stressed the word 'urgent'. It seemed like God had spoken, the great autonomous voice in the clouds, answerable to no one, and in complete control of all

36

instructions for life below.

At his interview Adam was told proudly that the American owners of Fix It turnover the same amount of money as the gross domestic product of a small developing country.

Adam had twice made his way across the store which was some quarter of a mile across. With the clock ticking, he broke into a half jog around an array of departments: paint, tiles, timber, home cleaning products, gardening tools, lawnmowers, power tools that only operate below 60db, laser-lined spirit levels, children's trampolines, sand pits, a small café, what looked like the baggage claim area for a regional airport, then over a fake 18th Century cobbled pavement towards a sofa area where people were reading novels, drinking coffee and eating muffins. Red totem poles were dotted around as 'meeting places', each with at least three people waiting with arms folded examining their watches, waiting for loved ones to reappear miraculously from behind metal shelf racks. Adam fell back into a bonsai tree display trying to avoid a rush of people marching towards the demo area for the next 'how-to'. He was still brushing the soil and needles from his trousers in the staff room.

A man of no less than seventy-five stood in front of a mirror rubbing Vaseline around his gums. Noticing Adam, he held his hand out. "Jim's the name, yes, yes." He had the far gone eyes of shell shock, and a quiet self-mocking chuckle after everything he uttered.

"I'm Adam. What do you do here, Jim?"

He rocked back on his heels and practiced his smile, testing just how far his lips could slide back. "Got to go, I'm the greeter at the front door today."

Adam was left alone with the steady heartbeat of the air conditioning, humming out like morning prayers as he put on his apron, the creases crisp and sharp. From the gallery of windows overlooking the shop floor, he gazed out at families moving through the crowds with ease, hands held like dad had instructed in the car park.

"So you're the new start?" a girl's voice suddenly said behind him.

A red-haired girl was sitting on a bench, her foot tapping in the air at an invisible accelerator pedal.

"I didn't mean to frighten you," she said. "I'm Cheryl as you can obviously see." She held out the name badge on her apron, which was stained with faint varnish spillages and threads loose and frayed from at least a year's service. Her style of makeup – the eyebrows artificially exaggerated, the eyes highly decorated – suggested she hadn't yet seen enough men in this, her late teens, to know the beauty of a painting isn't in touching it, but looking at it.

"It should say Adam. My name, I mean. My name is wrong…" Adam felt that inevitable blossoming of red on his cheeks, his own private Pompeii. "I'm not sure I'll find the tills. I got lost trying to get in here."

"Come on, then." She held out a motherly hand and took Adam downstairs. Her figure moved with the confidence that she was the shape she was going to be for most of her adulthood. Adam looked at her with the same wonderment as the girls two years above him in school, how much like adults they were getting. Cheryl made him feel like an inconsiderable boy.

At a hectic till area, a woman paced up and down, barking instructions at anyone in a red apron that happened to be in eyesight. She liked doing that: everyone who heard her shout would know she was in charge, as who else would be important enough to have to act so frantically. Every sentence finished in a higher registry than it had begun; everything was a warning of imminent disaster averted, thanks to her frequent hauntings and interventions. But she didn't always require to see what was going on. She had a radio microphone with a spittle-stained mouthpiece linking her to the security suite, where young men in brown shirts and ties stared into monitors showing every angle of the aisles. Through her radio she could operate the tannoy, and thus controlled the entire shop floor. Adam now recognised the voice of God he had heard upon entering. Her pallor spoke of lonely dinners eaten from her lap, of having the television schedule memorised the day before. She was very much in charge.

Adam put out his hand and introduced himself. "We spoke on the phone."

"You're on till three. Hold on…" She pressed the ear piece to hear reports of broken bulbs in Lighting. "No, don't do that! Of all the things you do, don't do that! We'll not be covered…" She raced off towards the trouble, leaving Adam alone at the tills with a growing circle of people demanding service.

Cheryl was talking with lively motions to a Timber Yard worker behind the customer service counter. Adam only picked up the occasional word about 'last night' and 'some other girl' which had clearly caused some friction between the two. The man was working hard to placate her; more promises were made that appeared to soften her mood. Then they tumbled back into the vacant security office, turning the blinds closed before falling against them, ruffling venetian, as M People's 'What Have You Done Today To Make You Feel Proud' played overhead. Adam's till was opened by a paunchy Bingo Hall-looking woman, and he was trying to remember what all the keys meant, instantly regretting being so high on cough syrup and rum on his training day.

The woman closed a stainless steel gate around his till, effectively locking him in. "It's a Health and Safety thing," she droned. Her spongy body didn't move, it fell about places, as influenced by a gust of wind from the garden centre than her own free will.

Customers swarmed to the till having scanned the numbered halo above Adam, then weighing up the speed of each queue, amounts waiting to be bought. They were just waiting for some failure in the consumer process: a till crash, a lack of carrier bags or change that could only be given in vouchers. For such material advocates of a system, they had a natural suspicion of it, that it couldn't keep *giving* like this forever. Was it really making them sick in other ways, ways that hadn't yet made themselves known? Did they not only talk in formalities: what they needed, when they had to have it done by, how much cheaper it was elsewhere, why that offer wasn't on anymore ('I was only here last week!').

The half bottle of Lambrini Adam had for breakfast had eased his transition from drug dealer to till operator with a pension contribution of twelve pence a week; the meeting of many of these people required much lubrication. Adam noticed how angry they all looked, shovelling money in and out of wallets, showing visible strain removing credit cards from their tiny overcrammed slats. They would buy, but they wouldn't be happy about it.

One man shifted his weight from foot to foot, looking around impatiently, trying to 'show' the world he was an important man with places to be. In fact, he was so busy he didn't have time to remove the plastic protective eye goggles from his forehead. No, he had to rush in and out. He was a man that did jobs! He wore a T-shirt that read, 'Whoever Dies With the Most Tools Wins.'

"Em…you know you still have your goggles on?" Adam said, juggling with the man's two packets of nails.

He patted down his bushy moustache, grimly reflecting on the statement. "I *know*."

"Would you like a bag, sir?"

He plucked the bags of nails in mid-flight. "Nah, just give em here."

"Thank you, then."

He snatched his receipt, unfamiliar with the pleasantry. Adam wondered what it must be like being that man, feeling the things he did, not being drunk or high in the daytime, or going to a party at night. Adam believed it to be simply terrible.

Chapter Four

'That punk kid'

The metal shutters crashed down behind Adam for the close of day. For everyone else it was drinking time, but seeing as he had been drinking throughout his entire shift, this hardly applied. The fountains spread out across the retail park all stopped spurting at the same time and small beacons lining the exit road lit up; God was pressing the buttons in the park management suite. But cars continued to roll into the car park, each with their windows down ready to bark out, "Hey pal, you guys closed?"

Adam looked back at the store, the shutters down, and shook his head. "No," he said and kept walking.

Cheryl walked ahead, hand in hand with the flannel shirt from the Timber Yard. They didn't speak to each other as they got in his Corsa on the other side of the car park, the slammed doors punctuating the silence leading up to it.

"Goodnight," Adam said to himself.

The bus spearing across the lanes of Union Street like it was on rails; this was a real ghost train, carrying lost souls to nights out, or rescuing others from the heady spin of happy hours only to dump them back in Paisley, where they suddenly longed for the pulse of the city again, where it felt roofless, and self examination didn't come quite so regularly or brutally. The driver was sitting in darkness – no passengers – a burning cigarette dangling from his mouth. The doors whooshed open and he grumbled for Adam to get on. The driver snatched his pass from him, and stared blankly at it, blowing a cloud of smoke over it. He looked back and forth between it and Adam's increasingly anxious face: a look of long gestated constipation. The driver's face was illuminated slightly by his cigarette, light creeping into the craters of pockmarks that chibbed his skin.

He quickly dropped the clutch and the bus lurched forward. Adam grabbed a handlebar and swung in to a seat. Realising it was too dark to roll a joint, Adam pleaded with the driver, "Hey man, can you turn the lights on…?"

They were careering down Jamaica Street, catching blinking amber lights. Adam stood up and analysed the unfamiliar passing streets. "Hey, man. Is this a shortcut or something?" They spun around a corner into a long straight, speed always gathering. Adam wrapped his arms and legs around a support pole like some terrified stripper, braced for a sudden halt that would want to send him through the front window.

They slowed, touring into some dark hovel estate, secluded, far from any prying eyes. This was where bad people went to escape the tyranny of CCTV cameras nearer the city centre. There were things going on out there that people would never know about, things that haunted old men upon seeing their grandchildren at Christmas time; things desperate women have done. For Adam, it would be a question from a bus driver that would live in his memory forever. It would be his one secret that he could absolutely never tell anyone, ever. Even if he knew he was going to die. With the nurse on her knees at the plug socket for his life support machine, he would remain steadfast and refuse to tell. Maybe if he was offered a drink, and he was already a little drunk, he would be tempted. Such sordid memories rarely pain quite so much when you have been anaesthetised with alcohol.

The engine switched off with a charcoal sigh, and there followed the same calm as when a neighbour's washing machine relents its spin cycle. Brilliant, thought Adam, someone will hear me scream now.

The driver's hand emerged out the cab to stub his cigarette out in the empty money tray. He got out and slammed the cab door much harder than seemed necessary.

Adam recoiled back in to his seat, sensing another confrontation with what Donald kept referring to as the Man. He pressed tight against the window. "Hey…hey, man. What's going on…"

The driver looked down. "I've seen you kids around. Around the Gallery." He was raspy. Adam was sure the man had never asked a woman to bed before. He would just suddenly lunge and the woman wouldn't bother getting up again. It's what happens to a voice when your reply to a question at work is to crank out a ticket from a machine. And that was how it came out. Like syntax or a fax. "So I was thinking, son, how about a wee blowjob?"

Adam noted the man had made no movement towards his groin yet, which at least indicated in the driver's mind this wasn't a done deal.

Then, as a window salesman throws out his closer line, so did the driver. "I can pay you." The only statement that would make Adam truly consider the proposition.

"Do I have to do it for you to take me back to the city centre? I think I want to get the train instead."

The driver didn't even complain or try to push him further. It was the actions of someone who had played this scene out on many

45

rainy October nights, and like the deflated gambler accepts his defeat with restrained petulance. He started up the engine again, the windows resuming their rattling, all the way to Govan where the bus swerved into a stop.

"That's you," the driver said.

"I'm going to Paisley," Adam shouted back, making sure to remain in his seat; as soon as he stood up he had given too much ground. The driver wouldn't really respect him for that. Adam tried to remember if the thumb went on the inside or the outside of a fist. Neither looked right to him.

"This is as far as I go," the driver shouted, looking straight out his windscreen.

"Bollocks! Sick of this bollocks." Adam got up wearily, with little sign of remaining defences, and walked towards the opening doors. "I'm calling Childline on you. Do you know what age I am? I'm calling Esther Rantzen on you."

The bus accelerated quickly, leaving Adam standing in a ankle-high puddle, surrounded by Halal butchers with their metal shutters down. Even ritually slaughtered meat kept a low profile at such a time. Shouts from gangs rang out around the circling tenement buildings, their voices bearing the timbre of Buckfast, the most vicious of wines. Soon they would funnel towards Adam on the main road, as wildebeest find canyons.

Adam set off for the only place he knew he was guaranteed a ride home at that time of night: the Gallery of Modern Art.

He could hear the gaggle of conversation about what drugs they thought the actors in Friends were on, and he knew he was safe. Tom, Dick, Harry, and Cherry looking as strung out as Adam had ever seen her.

"I want to get my hands on some Cerepan, I hear it's done wonders for Jody and her food cravings. What's she down to now?"

Tom launched a cigarette easily away and exhaled. "Six stone, I heard. Mind you, that was last week at Pepper's do, so I'd take off a pound a day knowing Jody."

The rain was dripping down from the monolithic pillars in gothic flourishes. Litter blew around the steps where the GOMA Kids had gathered, crisp packets circling their feet as if dreaming of long distance travel. Even without Cat, they remained stubbornly helpless.

Harry was already restless. He was squatting, his head facing down into his thighs, spitting out to the pavement, "I'm telling you lot, she's not coming." He turned to Cherry. "Why don't we just phone your dad?"

"He's away this week. Why don't you phone your dad?"

"Well he's not home, isn't he! What would be doing home at this ridiculous hour of night?" He rose to his feet and applauded slowly. "Oh thank god, here's Adam, at least he can give me one of those magic yellow things to calm me down."

Adam approached slowly, suspicious of the subtle compliment of his services. "Is Nicola around?"

He faced back towards the others, fluttering the tail of his coat. "That's who we're waiting on, too."

Dick was playing a Game Boy on the steps, Tom was leaning over his shoulder trying to direct him. From Tom's grimaces, he

47

wasn't doing Dick much good. The computer made a minor chord sequence, and Dick handed it to Tom. "I told her the Gallery, here, now, I don't know why she's not here. She's probably off with that guy again."

"Yeah, do any of you know who he is?" Adam asked.

"Only what she tells us, and that's not much. Can someone remind me what she does. I mean, she never does drugs with us anymore, she just wolfs them all down at home before she comes out."

Cherry started to protest. "Hey, Dick, calm down-"

"No, if she doesn't want to do drugs with us anymore, then what's the point? What is she going do?"

Tom spoke quietly to Adam as the others argued, his eyes narrow with concentration on the game. "You wanted to know about the boyfriend."

Adam sat beside him. "I just want to know where he gets his drugs from, just to make sure she's not getting shitty gear."

"Riiiight."

Just then an old Volkswagen Beetle limped towards the Gallery, headlights flickering.

Harry looked up into the rain and lit a cigarette. "Hallelujah!"

"Yes!" Tom yelled, his arms shooting up. "I'm on level three."

Cherry sat between Adam, with Harry and Dick on her other side. Tom demanded the passenger seat to concentrate further on the Game Boy. Cherry hadn't stopped talking since leaving ten minutes before.

"I mean, have you seen the pictures Helene was passing around. It was this biker guy, just random shots of this guy holding his helmet, and he's meant to be like her boyfriend. But she's not in like any of them. It's kind of sad really. I mean, not really, but if you were already feeling a bit sad when you heard it, then you might think about her for a second…"

Nicola still had remnants of a perfume scent in the car, too weak to have been recently applied, and just worn away enough to suggest it had rubbed off on someone. Cherry had jabbered her way into a gentle doze, her head falling into Harry's shoulder. Everyone tried to ignore the relentless passage of the motorway, the lights overhead passing monotonously through the car. Other vehicles took an age to pass them, allowing them to stare into the backseats full of suitcases ready for holidays, making their own journey seem that longer drawn out when all they wanted was to get home as fast as possible.

"Hey Adam," Harry asked, "did you hear about the Sharman Shapiro Ng novel I was telling you about? It just won the Booker Prize."

"I thought you said it was about nihilistic youth in America."

"It is."

"What was it called again?"

"'American Queers'."

"Wow. They mustn't like that."

"You're kidding. They're going crazy for it other there! I love how he tells you exactly what it's like to be American and really pissed off."

"Where's he from?"

"Manchester. Like I said, now he's won the Booker Prize, it's too late to like it, because if you like it now, then you're just another machine that's fallen for the hype of the prize."

"But it won."

He paused, genuinely confused. "I know that, but I read it before it won."

Nicola tried to coax some conversation from Tom, but he was too immersed in his game of Italian plumbers and talking mushrooms to speak. Her eyes met Adam's in the rear view mirror occasionally; she used the excuse of a roundabout to look longer than was required; she noted his eyes bulging from lack of sleep, exhausted like an overfed stomach. The motorway fractured into Paisley, the now frequent stabs on the brake jarring after the smoothness and consistent speed of the motorway.

"What street are you again, Adam?" Nicola asked.

"Caledonia Street, round from the Sheriff Court."

"Oh, that's handy," Dick said.

"Yeah, Dick," Harry laughed, "I hear there's an STD clinic just down the road as well."

"Did you hear that, Harry, that was the sound of no one laughing except yourself."

"Piss off, you child." He looked to Adam. "You won't believe it, I caught this guy listening to the fucking Doors last week. Next he'll be telling us that Pink Floyd were better after Syd Barrett left."

Dick yelped, "They were!"

Nicola surveyed the desolate scene of scarred fronts of the tenement buildings that lined the street. The others went quiet; they didn't normally have to think about where Adam might live; as long as he delivered. Edward had told Adam a story about his brother

Patrick who was working somewhere very big in finance down in London. When they went out to clubs, church people would hijack him and his friends in the bathrooms with pictures of South Americans working in terrible conditions to make them their cocaine. In a way, the others always knew, even since school, when his packed lunch would come wrapped in a Farmfoods carrier bag, where theirs were always Sainsbury's or Marks and Spencer.

"Which one is yours?" Nicola asked.

Adam pointed to the window with no curtains; a pile of cigarette butts lay around the street directly under his window.

Nicola spoke through her open window. "Cat said you were coming to 'Commit Suicide'."

"Yeah," Adam nodded.

"Cool." Nicola revved the engine, ready to pull away.

"Hey, where is Cat anyway?"

Harry poked his head through the rear window as the car took off again. "No one knows. We thought you did."

Upstairs, the bathroom mirror offered Adam little sanctuary, disappointing him in looking worse than he felt. He stripped to his underwear and observed the ragged canvas he was becoming. He looked beyond his seventeen years, his muscles light and haggard, well worn. He took a razor blade from behind his toothbrush, and readied it at his chest. "How can you be so fucking ugly?" he said and dragged it across his left pectoral, just above three thin, whitening scars. He had sliced a few light hairs the last time which dried in against his skin when the blood went chalky. Two sheets of toilet paper blotted the cuts, then he retired to bed.

It had been nearly a month since he had last masturbated; the act itself had turned into an ugly biological chore, best saved for the dark, under the covers. The solitude of living alone actually lessened his desire to do it. He lay still for a minute, contemplating it. He sat up and slammed down a few Seroxat. His first solid all day. The photo made its regular journey to Adam's lips and then back to the wall. The pillows caught him satisfactorily on the way down: he was a little ashamed, embarrassed, and unsatisfied. But at least he was high.

Chapter Five
"A Drunk Man Looks at the Thistle"

Each of the buildings at Thistle University looked like a Radisson hotel, the kind they put up next to major airports. All metal hand rails, clean lines and large functional pieces of abstract art. Long runways intertwined like small motorway systems around campus.

Adam's dad had been dead against it from the start:

"How much is this going to cost me?"

"Nothing, dad."

"What are you studying?"

"English."

"Waste of fucking time, if you ask me..."

Adam wasted time inventing fictional back stories of his life, mostly involving his mother. He could picture her scenes so vividly it didn't even feel like lying; as honest as a dirty dream; as untrue as a stranger's embrace, as he had found another reason to go to university: he was making £150 a week from selling goods stolen from lockers and unattended bags. It was a pure, New Britain enterprise, with buyers handing Adam lists of items they wanted whilst sitting back to back on the marble bench outside the library.

In the toilets there was the usual queue for the mirrors where several guys were lined up sculpting their hair to messy perfection, gossiping sordidly.

"...so then Max says, 'no way, she's too young...'" The sound of a line being snorted rose up from under the door. "but hey, if there's grass in the field..."

Adam was already late for his lecture, so he tapped ever so

tentatively on the cubicle door.

"Please fuck off right away!" came the instant response.

"I'm sorry but, I'm late for a lecture and the urinals are blocked. Could you maybe…do that outside?"

There was no reply, so Adam waited for them to finish. When the boys emerged, they swaggered with confidence, but their white pallor made them look sluggish, struggling through the heavy air.

Adam closed the cubicle door, and noticed a white residue still sitting on the cistern. It was thin, spread out, but swept together with his library card made a decent line. He wasn't sure what it was at first – probably too early for coke – until the rush collided with his heart on the way out the building, the unmistakable warmth of speed.

The lecture hall was only half-full, with fifty or so students scattered evenly around. Adam stood and observed them for a minute, to gauge where he could sit to avoid much notice of his nervous energy. A row appeared like Swiss neutrality to him, but he wouldn't be able to sneak in entirely unnoticed. The back door creaked open slowly and loudly, causing the furthest back rows to turn round. He murmured an apology, then a gust of wind slammed the door shut behind him, blowing everyone's notes off their tables. Adam shut his eyes and felt his face burn like Dante's Inferno, the ghouls in front of him staring.

Dr Arnott shouted, "Glad you could join us, Adam," and adjusted the next acetate the wind had blown off his overhead projector. "Why don't you come to the front?" he said cheerily. Adam could tell Arnott had already had a few.

Adam's bag caught the armrest of an empty chair of the front row and pulled it over, causing a loud metallic crash. He struggled with the chair, folding then unfolding it again, trying to work out how it stood.

"Just leave that, I'll get it later," said Bob, with the tone of someone that had seen Adam fuck up in public before.

Adam mouthed "sorry" to each person as he bumped his way into the middle of the row, as the lecture continued. Then the small desktop under the seat wouldn't unravel. Adam kept pulling on it but it wouldn't budge. Bob struggled to be heard over the squeaking and scraping of the chair on the linoleum floor. With one last pull he yanked the desk out, sending his folder with all his lecture notes into the air. They seemed to take forever to glide down and land on the heads of the people on either side of him.

Adam rested his hands on his lap, whispering, "I'll just get them at the end."

At the back row were two boys Adam's age sitting at the back door like long-lost relatives at a funeral, observing his awful entrance. They were dressed formally: both in expensive pinstripe suits and carrying brown canes, the light shining off the lacquer. Strange, but as the lecture went on, Adam felt that they were looking not just to the front, but specifically at himself. He sat uneasily in his chair, turning round every so often, much to the annoyance of the person directly behind him. "Want a photograph, Oliver Twist?" he asked.

The boy's electronic organiser lay within reach on top of his bag, surrounded by two tubs of hair gel, one for emergency's, Adam presumed. He spent the next ten minutes of the lecture working out how many ounces of weed he could buy with it. So he let a sheet of notes fall over the bag and quietly scooped it up. Arnott paused for a second, peering over his notes at Adam.

Of course, he justified his petty criminalities in many ways: "they can afford it" "they probably never used it anyway" "they won't even notice". Ultimately, Adam felt he was righting some metaphysical wrong, that bearing the absence of any real God, he himself would take care of judgment. He only stole from those he had heard speak or act in a displeasing manner – racism, misogyny, homophobia, superficiality – and in those few seconds, he would decide whether or not they deserved to go without something themselves. It was hard for him not to feel that he had already been a victim of a different sort of theft.

Adam even thought of writing to Tony Blair about his escapades: *"he might be proud of my industry. Maybe I'll send him a letter and tell him, and he'll invite me to Downing Street to meet Richard Branson and Noel Gallagher."*

Bob's lecture was the start of a module on Scottish literature and poetry – that week, Hugh MacDiarmid. "…and founder of the National Party of Scotland, later of course renamed the Scottish National Party. So, does anyone have any thoughts on MacDiarmid from the reading I gave you last week?"

The room fell silent then the back door clattered shut again. The boys in the suits were gone.

He raised his hand tentatively.

"Yes, Adam?"

"Well, he wrote using a lot of Scottish dialects."

"Mm, mm. And what did he discuss in his work?"

He started so gingerly, terrified that if allowed to speak for more than ten seconds, they wouldn't be able to shut him up. He cleared his throat, "excuse me. I think it's like what Alexander Trocchi said...the whole Scottish *scene* if you like...it's all bollocks."

A few people broke into giggles at the front.

Bob paced from one side of the room to the other. "What a delightful insight, Adam. Wish to elaborate?"

More giggling.

The speed had won; he couldn't hold back any longer, feeling an ease come over him that wouldn't otherwise have been accessible, the best reason for doing drugs that Adam could think of. "Well, what I mean is, it's all that tired, triumph-of-the-Scottish-spirit shit. It's all very good talking about the purple heather and rolling mountains, but who lives surrounded by that? Who gets to live in such idyllic circumstance? No one. Or hardly anyone. You can't just deny anything that isn't irrevocably joyful. We don't all live in cottages staring at a fireplace, drinking whisky, singing songs about how great it is to not have central heating; we live in domestic violence and casual alcoholism; we don't improve ourselves, we just consume more; we don't see ourselves as part of the world, we're all stubborn, rank little isolationists, when the universe is expanding at sixteen thousand miles a day. You get the feeling that if we could go to the outer reaches of space, we couldn't be bothered. Well Alex Trocchi wanted to travel out there, and so do I."

God, Adam thought, I feel like having a drink. Just a wee one.

Bob paced back across the floor to his lectern and looked around the room at eyes thrown towards the ceiling, heads bursting with hangovers from last night's parties. Those boys with their legs recklessly agape, caveman-style, always so conscious of being men; those girls with their stomachs in knots from late periods and pregnancy strips turning blue.

Bob drank persistently from a mug on his lectern, filled with whisky. He rarely did a lecture sober. "So are you saying, Scotland is just an idea?"

"It's just people, alone, trying to survive, tossed out like satellites into space. That was Trocchi's beef: he just saw people, one consciousness, but MacDiarmid saw a smaller struggle." Adam was surprised: he had finally produced the same drug babble he had heard from junkies at his dealer Duke's house, and thought so impressive.

Bob nodded with a quick look at his watch. "I think we'll pick this up tomorrow. In the meantime I want you to read Trocchi's 'Cain's Book', of which there are plenty of copies set aside in the library."

Everyone slowly trickled out and Adam picked up the rest of his lecture notes from the floor. Bob's shadow loomed over him and he handed him a stray page, not noticing a picture of a matchstick man swinging from a hanging tree in the top corner.

"You look a damn mess, Adam."

"Thanks."

He handed Adam a stack of his files and folders which piled up just past Adam's eyes. "I cancelled your essay meeting for tomorrow. There's been a lot of drinking in the Post Modernity class, so I have to go supervise. Why don't you walk me to the office and we'll rearrange."

Adam sensed he was about to get 'a talk', an intervention.

Classes poured out into the corridors, papers falling off the top of the pile as Adam dodged in and out of the students.

"Come on, Adam, keep up!" he said, sliding through the crowd with his whisky lubrication. Drink has that effect, the ease of movement.

Adam brushed the hair from his eyes and ran to catch up. Going through a set of swing doors, an old man shouted after Bob.

"Professor Bernstein," Bob said. "How's life on the third floor?"

The man's plush east coast accent relished every syllable. "Arnott, I missed you at my reading last night. Kelman was there!" He pulled out a pink polka dot hankie – matching his tie and suit lining – and blew his bulbous purple nose loudly and brashly. "And who's this eager young buck?"

Buck, Adam thought. He had never been called that before.

Bob said, "Philip, this is Adam," trying to pull him away as subtly as possible.

Bernstein shook his hand and bowed slightly. His hand was cold and sweaty, almost post-coital, and he held on uncomfortably long. "Pleasure. *Pleasure.*" He finally stopped gazing into his eyes and nodded a goodbye to Bob, before strutting away like Oscar Wilde, parting the swing doors with grace.

Bob strode away, saying, "God, I thought he was going to pull you into the broom cupboard there. He must like the delicate looking ones."

"I'm not delicate am I, Bob?"

He sniggered as he tried to unlock the office door, missing the lock several times. "No, no I don't think so." He sat at his desk, leafing through old Red Wedge leaflets as he fixed them some drinks, kicking over some glass bottles in his private washroom. A picture of a twenty-something girl sat facing Adam. He had constructed different stories about the girl each time he visited Bob. The most likely was an old love, lost, perhaps, tragically. Tragedy always made more sense to Adam.

"You know, I've been talking to your other lecturers and advisors," Bob said.

"And what did they have to say?" Adam's thoughts had already turned to what he was going to buy from the off-licence on the way home.

"You're failing everything apart from my English modules. You're going to have to be careful, Adam. You've only been here a month, but make no mistake, they *will* kick you out if you don't improve. You're bottom of the class so far, grade wise."

"Is that why you asked me to come up here?"

He sat down across from Adam, offering him a mug. "Coffee?"

"Make it Irish, heavy on the Irish."

He poured some Whyte and Mackay into a mug for him. They both took long drinks, comfortable in the presence of a fellow boozer. "It's…complicated," he said. "I might be leaving, to concentrate on my novel…"

"What? But you can't do that!" Adam yelled. "What am I meant to do?"

"Calm down. It's not going to be forever. I just need until the end of the year, and I'll be back for the next semester in the New Year."

"How about a scribe, or a research assistant. Do you need me around to help with things?"

Bob downed the rest of his mug then immediately refilled it.

"Dad," Adam began, then froze in horror at his mistake. "Oh Christ, you're going to throw Freud down on me now, aren't you?"

"What I should do is throw fucking Dickens at you! Or, ideally, Dostoevsky, but I don't think you can handle any more human misery. It's like watching 'Crime and Punishment'. Speaking of which."

Adam got a lump in this throat.

"What did you pinch from that moron's bag during the lecture?"

"Electronic organiser," he said blankly. "What can I say, the only thing that guy ever reads is the instructions on bottles of Rohypnol."

"That may very well be the case, but you need to give me it. I'll hand it in to Lost Property."

Adam wasn't really drinking the whisky anymore, he just let it lap up to his closed lips.

"You don't seem to speak much to the other students. A month and I haven't seen it, except to argue with someone at the back of the class. Calling anyone who doesn't agree with your thoughts on Jean Baudrillard a fascist."

"Some of them are fascists, Bob! You don't hear what these people talk about. It's like the Third Reich in Topman outfits, all drunk on vodka and Red Bull. There's no limit to who they will humiliate in order to fell better about themselves. There no rules with them when it comes to satisfaction."

Bon paused to determine if Adam was finished. "Can you just stop this stealing? There's nothing I can do if you carry that on."

"Are you depressed, Bob?"

He sighed and rolled his eyes. "I teach English for a living, of course I'm bloody depressed."

"Because I think I'm depressed too. Just stay a few more months and drink with me. You can write a novel about it and it'll win prizes. What's the one you're writing about?"

"I suppose it's about grief, losing someone."

Adam nodded, pulling his lips together to a point. "Not very cheery."

"No, I suppose not. It's probably the booze that makes me think of melancholy. I never understood that drinking to celebrate. It was always just a release for me.

"I can't imagine drinking when you're happy. Must be bloody awful." Adam noticed the pause between them, and so stood up and walked towards the door. He wished there was filing cabinet edge on which to steady his rocking self. Drinking at such a time of the morning is like being a little boy on a scooter, pushing and pushing and pushing, legs burning – all just for those several yards of grace with his legs held up off the ground, sliding unaided by anything but the turning of the world. It seems worth all the effort for those several yards.

He looked back with his hand on the door. "They think I'm fucking melanoma, the other students. I won't last long here. It's not what I thought it would be. There's just more of the same here as everywhere else, only it hurts more here, because this was meant to be my sanctuary, a safe place to escape the banality and mediocrity of the outside world you talked about in your first lecture. Come on, you know there's something wrong with the world, don't you. It doesn't make sense that so many people can wander around so miserable looking and sounding, and keep doing what they're doing. I just know that we could all be happier but…"

"You just can't say how."

"Right."

Bob pointed at Adam with his mug. "You should read MacBeth. It seems like the right time for you."

"MacBeth?"

He nodded. "The Scottish Play…I know about your mum, Adam, and I know you don't live at home anymore."

"How do you know all this?"

"It's on your application."

"For admittance purposes only, it says."

"Well, this is technically an admittance issue."

"What's your point?"

"I'm pretty sure how you could be happier. You're going to have to start dealing with things, if you know what I mean."

Adam smiled assuredly. "I deal very well."

Chapter Six
'The Crooked Saltire'

Adam denied to himself that it was loneliness that brought him to the doors of his dad's pub, The Crooked Saltire, that night. He slalomed through the retiring shoppers of the day, and their fistfuls of carrier bags, faces tight with effort. The half bottle of vodka Adam drank earlier had dulled his nerves. "Christ," he said, facing the battered chipboard door entrance.

No one paid much attention to Adam's entrance. A television no one was watching played loudly behind the bar – but very little else moved, except the rising and falling of a smoking- or drinking-hand. The patrons had run out of words to describe their experiences.

"Another?"

"Aye. Why not."

Davie Bernadette, Adam's father, was pouring coins into the '£20 Jackpot' slot machine, nestling a pint glass and a lit cigarette in the other hand – even with his shoulders back and stomach sucked in, the machine dominated him like a lover. From where Adam stood, a screen above his father flashed with an icon saying '£20', appearing to put a price on his head. Everything on his body seemed to come from his endless jaw, all his exaggerated motions desperately trying to convey power, even if he was just lighting another cigarette. After taking his first puff, he would tear it from his lips, extending his arm away from his body in sharp motion, as if throwing a dart. These marking-out rituals were also carried out at the bar, throwing down his packet of Benson and Hedges next to his glass, laying down a perimeter that couldn't be breached.

Frank took a look over Davie's shoulder to see what was coming next on the wheels. "Another Tennent's, Alison," shouted Frank towards the bar, causing Davie to step back at the sudden noise.

"Well done, Frankie, ah just hit the wrong button."

"Give it a rest, Davie," said Alison, the Geordie bar keep. She had large breasts, which were more and more convinced by gravity every day. The wives hated her because they knew she was what their husbands thought about during sex, all the pub scenarios working out in their heads.

"Your wife called for you...*again*," Alison said.

Frank collided with the bar, spraying his loose change into the crop circles of spilled lager and cider.

The slot machine played a diminuendo chorus and Davie bellowed, "Aw, fuck me. Frank, ah'm gonna need more change an all. *Aye*, I want another pint! D'you think this is."

"Aright Dad," Adam said, tentative to approach. He had been bad luck last time: six months ago. There was a pause to look at him, then his father's hand disappeared into his pocket for the last of the pound coins, his face returning to the three wheels.

Adam glanced at the five empty glasses sitting on top of the puggy machine.

He laughed through the cloud of smoke he had just exhaled. "D'you want me to tell Alison you're here?"

"Why would I want you to do that?" Adam asked, already blushing at seeing her.

"No reason."

"Sorry I've not been around. I've been busy."

"Busy? Aye, it's a shame when you're busy. Cannae get fuck all else done."

"Did you go to the Job Centre today?"

He ignored the question and shouted, "Where's that fucking pint!"

Frank was still leering at Alison as she leant over the glass washer, the steam rising out the top, her white blouse almost see-through to her bra.

"Well," she announced, giving Frank the eye. "I'd better go check the bogs are clean." She left the bar and Frank followed her into the men's.

The last of the money had run out, so Adam and his father were left alone, except for the television playing between them. Adam still had his hands in his pockets as he had arrived.

"What's the matter, you not drinking?"

"I'm fine."

"Why you not drinking? Have a drink for fuck's sake. I've no seen you in weeks."

"Has it been that long, I never realised."

"What's the matter, you no well? Have a drink."

"I'll get one in a minute when Alison comes back."

"Thirty seconds I should think, knowing Frank." He took another dart throw of his cigarette, puffing out all over Adam. "Still hanging around with that fucking Professor? He's a weird one, that. Aw they books."

"What's so weird about books?"

"Just seems weird, that's all!" he said looking up gormlessly at the news playing. "It's no way to earn a living. He's an old man."

"He's the same age as you." With no sign of the men's toilet door stirring, Adam poured himself a beer, leaning over the bar to reach the tap.

"Well at least I can say you've inherited my thirst. I was getting worried there."

Adam tumbled in to a stool. "You pick up your benefits last week?"

"Aye! How?"

"Just wondering. I thought I saw you when I was on the bus with Eddie."

"Oh aye. He away home yet?"

"Yeah."

"Ah should really phone your Uncle Patrick."

"Why? What do you have to say to each other?"

"No much, ah suppose."

Adam stared at the TV behind the bar, the news playing inaudibly. "So how much do you need to put in before you win the twenty pound jackpot?" he asked.

"That's not the point."

The picture suddenly jumped to a six-month-old still of Tony Blair outside Downing Street with hysterical Union Jacks lining his entry, then to his address outside church for Princess Diana's funeral. Adam remembered seeing people huddled together in front of the windows of electrical stores, the different sized televisions showing her coffin being driven down the motorway. Adam's father had changed channels in their living room, complaining, "Christ, you'd think she was the only person that ever died."

Davie tried lighting a cigarette but he went into a coughing fit, doubling over. His face turned bright red, like he was hacking up oil, until finally he stopped and the blood drained from his face. He lit a cigarette and sighed, "Oh, that's fucking better!"

They stood in silence as he picked at his teeth then rolled enough cigarettes to cover the next few hours, stopping every few moments to hack his guts up again. Adam took his father's Rizla and rolled a few of his own. Now armed with a fresh pocketful of change Frank had left him, Adam's father turned his body back to the slot machine, talking directly over his shoulder to him. Like a setting sun, on its perpetual axis, he came to Adam, then moved away. But for a moment he would be Adam's, at afternoon-high.

The toilet door flew open and out stepped Alison, slightly flushed and her hair ruffled. She went back behind the bar and carried on with her duties after reapplying her cheap lipstick. A few seconds later, Frank came out, his shirt untucked at the back.

"Frank, where the fuck have you been?"

He laughed. "Just keeping the Scottish end up, know whit a mean, Davie…"

Adam finished his drink and tapped a five pound note on the Tennent's header. "Please, Alison."

Frank said, "Awright, Adam, it's been a few weeks."

"No, six months, apparently." Adam gestured to the corner of his mouth. "You've still got a bit of lipstick…"

The machine played another diminuendo chorus and his dad yelled, "Shite. Did you get ma pint, Frank?"

The stubbed out fags were piled high in the ashtray next to Adam. He spun it like a top, watching the ash flakes overflow, disappearing in their spiral down towards the floor. Alison was now hanging over the bar at his father, lingering and laughing at his jokes with exaggerated, mischievous shrieks.

Frank retired to a table of silent men sitting in the corner of the room, each staring blankly at the television.

Adam was left alone – he took such a hard drink the lager swashed up to his nostrils, leaving a foamy tide which he quickly wiped away with the sleeve of his overcoat. His glass shuddered on the wooden bar as he left to stand by the outside doors and watch the sun fall. The sudden brightness outside had left no hint in the windowless pub: their only light was artificial. Adam could find no sunset song.

A fat woman ambled past him with a load of Poundshop carrier bags and he instinctively reached out to her in a fit of humanity, offering her a hug, reasoning she must be feeling the same things as he was. She waved him off hard, jabbering hysterically, "you're mad," and wobbled away.

Adam called after her, "I'm sorry. I just thought…"

Adam's father lit a cigarette, slumping against the bar next to his son, both with the same kink in their left leg. "So whit's the fucking script?"

"What do you mean?" Adam asked, finally breaking his gaze at the foam of yet another pint.

"Whit you doing here?"

"I don't need a reason."

"Aye you do. It's Friday Night Football on Sky in half an hour."

He took a long hard draw on his cigarette. "Well, I'll be damned…they do like their mindless distractions."

"I don't know whit your fucking problem is. It's nice in here. You get a nice pint, bit of telly, what's not to like?" He gestured around the walls, stained brown with tobacco and the worn down red and blue Paisley patterned carpet.

"Why would I want to come here? It's like a morgue."

Alison appeared, trying to reach through the crowd of glasses the pair had collected, to empty the ashtray which was presently spilling over.

"Just leave it will you."

She retreated quickly with a head shake.

"Look, let's just drink our fucking drinks and forget the whole fucking thing!" He sighed. "Billy…you know Billy that lives down the stairs from you…he says he heard you fucking throwing stuff around your flat the last few nights. Glasses smashing, thumping noises on the walls…You better keep it down."

Adam hesitated for a moment then said unconvincingly, "He's…lying."

"How were you throwing things round your flat?"

"Why was I throwing things round my flat?" This was a trait of Adam's that had bugged his father, trying to improve his sentences for him. He flicked his cigarette constantly until there was no ash left. "I'll tell him sorry. I didn't mean for anyone to hear. I just couldn't sleep, alright? I haven't been sleeping properly so I thought it would do some good to let some energy out. It was just an accident with the television. It got stuck on a channel Eamonn Holmes was on and I just had to beat the shit out of something."

"He says he heard you screaming. Shouting things about yourself. Whit…whit's all that about…"

Adam's dad was drunk was now drunk beyond any sense, swaying back and forth on his stool. He slurred, "…maybe we could be mates again…we used to have a laugh…d'you remember…"

"Mates?" Adam took one last draw of his fag. "Are we done? Can I go now? Because I've got *mates* coming over tonight, Dad." He was lying. "I…I don't know what you *want* from me," he said stabbing his cigarette furiously in the ashtray.

"You been to see Doctor Hume again?"

"Yes."

"He phoned me a wee while ago. We had quite a talk…quite a long talk about you. He says you're drinking too much. I mean, I tried to tell him, look doc, it's only natural for a boy to want to blow off some steam now and then. It's no hurt me any."

"What does it matter?" Adam asked, just desperate to leave.

"When was the last time you were at the cemetery?"

Adam paused, seeing months pass by, snow appearing than vanishing, making way for sun, twice over. He shook his head gently. "I don't remember."

The two looked at each other, unsure of how else to end it, so Adam walked towards the door, Alison leaning back over the bar.

She whispered to Davie, "I was just going to go clean the toilets again, if you want to come."

"Pour me another pint first. The football's on soon."

Adam mumbled to himself, "Friday. Something I was supposed to remember…"

Chapter Seven

'The Fur King'

Adam tumbled off the bus, his feet kicking out into a manic run, his white socks gleaming in the dark. He was quickly in the heart of an industrial landscape – so soon from the suburbs – where the land was sprinkled with 'In Development' and 'For Sale' signs, ready for housing projects, cinemas, and restaurants, part of the growing River Oak complex. He followed the noise of late night traffic rushing across the flyover nearby, the red taillights swooping and vanishing, as if being swallowed by a concrete wave.

Across the other side of the park, standing imperious in the falling snow, above the white matchsticks of the parking places, a large balloon-type figure stood on top of the Fur King building, swaying in the breeze next to the multi-storey car park.

Adam stumbled across the car park, his shoes beating hard and unbending against the concrete which glistened with frost. A neon sign beamed in bright lights above Adam, 'The Fur King. Where prices are Fur-King low!' The brightness was painful for Adam's timid eyes, making the metal shutter in front of him glow in alternating primary colours.

"Donald," he said, tapping hesitantly on the shutter door.

A sharp whistle rang out from the roof. Straining to see up through the snow, Adam saw Donald hanging over the edge of the shop roof, waving him towards the adjacent roof of the multi-storey car park.

He followed the winding ramps up to the top floor which was open top. The howling wind drove the snow in almost horizontally at

75

Adam, who could just about make out Donald waving him to jump over to his side. Adam leapt over the gap – the length of a body and a sheer drop of forty feet to the concrete below – between the two buildings.

The two boys were dwarfed by the giant inflatable Fur King. (He was a fat man that looked like Trotsky, with a ridiculous gold crown and fur coat wrapped around him, his five metre smile beaming out into the night).

Adam shouted over the wind that was gusting to gale force, "Donald, what am I doing up here?"

He had his typical stoned drawl. "Horrible night isn't it?"

"No." Adam looked to the heavens. "It's fucking glorious!"

Donald held out his hand. "What happened, man? I've been waiting up here freezing my nads off."

Adam slapped it away and barked, "Can we get in out of this fucking gale, first?"

They descended a deep staircase from under the Fur King, to a corridor lined with lights at waist height, stretching as far as you could see. Water dripped down rusted brown pipes, reams of wires sparking above them as they walked past., one almost hitting us both as it dangled.

"Donald, where the hell are we going?"

"Just wait. It won't be long now."

They continued through a complex series of twisting corridors and locked doors, until they reached a sign that read, "Shop floor access. Security personnel only."

Donald pulled out a series of keys and unlocked the door of a maintenance lift. He pushed the up button and paced around, giggling excitedly to himself. "Did you bring those yellow ones we had last time?"

Adam examined his eyes in the mirror panel on the wall. "I brought the yellow ones. And the pink ones. Everything Cat asked for."

The lift stopped and as the doors opened, Donald said, "Party time."

They stepped out and the lift doors shut with a ping. They were in the middle of the River Oak Shopping Centre. Everything was bathed in the dark green light of the centre's backup generator – which was still, somehow, powering the escalators. Some shop fronts smouldered with fire, and in a large fountain, the water surface was bubbling in flames.

"What the hell have you idiots done?" Adam asked.

"It was my idea to fill the fountain with petrol," Donald said proudly, walking towards the escalators. Underneath them were the silhouettes of a group of twenty people sitting around a pile of rucksacks.

"Cameras," Adam said to Donald, pointing around the ceiling.

"No power," he replied, holding up ring of switchboard keys.

"Security guards."

"Not until they figure out a way to get the power back on."

Adam stood beside the fountain, passing his hand back and forth over the flames. "Cat? Are you here?"

She peeked out at first then ran out from under the escalators and threw her arms around Adam. "Oh, I knew you would come!" She smelled of cider. "Did you bring the yellow ones?"

"Yes, I've explained to Donald, already."

She had been scribbling into a notepad, carefully documenting the chaos. "The magazine's gonna love this stuff."

"You're drunk."

"I feel like Harper Lee."

"You're very drunk."

The rest of the group sat hunched under the escalators and passed joints around, a portable CD player was playing Cat's Portishead album. They were all dressed in black hoodies and T-shirts, the floor littered with bongs and pipes, and blue carrier bags from the off licence; the empties strewn across the floor. 'GOMA Kids' had been spray painted on every available surface.

A voice spoke from under the escalators. "Donald said you would come."

"Is that you, Bug?" Adam asked.

The boy slugged from a half bottle of whisky then lobbed it into the fountain, sending a quick burst of flames into the air. "This is a shit party."

Adam laughed, tossing some vials towards Cat. "As requested. Can I go now?"

"You should stay for a while," Donald said.

Bug said in a weed-rasped croak, "I can think of worse places to get stoned, you know. We've got the donut and cookie shops over there."

Fiona was sitting next to him. Maybe it was the green light, but her cheekbones seemed even more prominent than the last time Adam had seen her.

He ran his hands aggressively through his hair. "I'll be honest," he said, "I'm really drunk; I'm freezing cold; I'm not in the mood."

Bug's face seemed transparent, a negative. "We should have gone to my house instead. It's sitting there empty just now."

"So's mine," Fiona said.

"God, you're so lucky," Cat added, "my mum's back home tomorrow."

"Look, how long do you think it's going to take for them to get the power back on and realise something's wrong?" Adam asked.

Donald shook his head. "Hours. We'll be long gone by then. They probably won't even notice anything until they do a walk round in the morning."

Adam dipped a cigarette into the fire on the fountain and sat on the stationary escalator. "So, how's the story coming along, Cat?"

She leaned towards him, eyelids fluttering in distress. "It's like totally…malignant."

"Malignant?"

"Yeah, you know, like fashionable and cutting edge at the same time." Cat waited to see how impressed Adam would be.

"I don't think that's what it means, Cat." Adam padded his coat down for cigarettes. "Do you think I'm allowed to smoke in here?"

"Probably. Some dude called Sky over there turned all the cigarettes on the warning signs into penises, so it's really just blowjobs that are illegal in here."

Adam noticed a pair of legs stretched out over a girl's shoulders, buried in a cage of footballs in Sports Universe. "Someone better tell *them*, then."

Some Kids were trudging from shop to shop, filling up their rucksacks with designer dresses and armfuls of accessories, but mostly there were sprawled out on the floor in X-shapes beside decapitated mannequin heads. A couple were slow-dancing under a mirror ball in the Gadget Shop, both clutching bottles of Mad Dog 20/20, taking slurps over the other's shoulder before braving another messy kiss, with teeth occasionally chinking upon their lips touching, so eager to get inside, to feel that warm, wet other-world of a stranger's tongue. The boy kept his eyes open when he kissed. He didn't want to look gay.

From the escalator, Adam could see Cat's notepad, documenting who had paired off into what shop, with words like 'blowjob? Sensationalise.' circled. A boy crawled over with a CD held delicately in his hand. "What are you doing?" Cat shrieked.

"I was going to put on Sonic Youth," the boy chirped back.

"Oh please, that's so…so…" Cat looked around, realising she had no one to finish her sentence for her.

The generator suddenly cut out and the centre went pitch black.

"What…the fuck…" Donald wailed, now wearing a tweed hat from Marks and Spencer.

Cat sulked, "Donald, what the fuck are you wearing? You look like an old man."

Bodies came rushing out of the shops, still putting their clothes back on, makeup smudged, shoes untied. They stood paralysed, waiting for something to move or make a sound. Somewhere outside, heavy doors were being slammed, footsteps running across the catwalk

80

above the shops. Torches flashed down and radios buzzed with static either side of some inaudible instruction.

The lights overhead spluttered on, prompting shrieks from some, sighs from others before lying back down on the ground, too blissed or spaced to move or realise what was happening.

"Right, everyone stay where you are," a voice from above demanded.

Donald dropped his hand on Adam's shoulder. "I'll be honest, man, I'd really appreciate it if you got us out of this shit."

Cat – who had decided in the absence of the dark green light to reapply her mascara – added, "If my watch is right, Adam, I will be sober in approximately half an hour. Let's not have that happen."

Adam pushed them forward. "Follow me," he said, and took them towards the lifts Donald had brought him up in.

Fiona and Bug, who had only just stopped kissing and realised what was happening, leapt up and followed them.

Cat looked back and screeched, "No, my Portishead CD!"

"I'll get you another," Adam replied.

Donald held on to his hat as he tried to keep pace.

"Wait for us," yelled Fiona, whose legs looked like they might snap with the impact of her running. Bug sauntered along behind, stopping to light a massive joint.

They passed a couple sleeping by the entrance to the Food Court, a chequered table cloth doing for a duvet.

Adam continually battered the 'down' button, feeling the weight of cannabis and alcohol heavy in his chest. In fact, they were all bent double, leaning on their knees, coughing and howling like grizzled veterans, not an ounce of vitality in their cheeks. Bug looked at them in confusion. "Anyone want a pass of this?"

Everyone said 'yeah' and filled the waiting lift.

The security guards desperately tried to round up the GOMA Kids left behind as best they could, but they kept throwing up or collapsing in drunken waste.

Cat stared at the passing floor numbers on the door panel in disillusion, arms folded, refusing to speak.

"What's the matter?" Donald enquired, trying to prise her arms apart.

She pulled back, violently. "Don't touch me. Unless it's to give me another Portishead CD. I swear to god I'll fucking FREAK OUT if I don't have a new one by tomorrow. It's my come down album."

"I'm sure your dad will get you another one," Adam suggested.

The lift was rapidly filling with smoke from Bug's joint. Everyone was trying to take as much as possible from without it being obvious on the next pass, but Cat was taking long draws of it, oblivious that Bug was staring at her, waiting for it back. "And my notes. I don't even have the story for the magazine."

Fiona smiled, draped against a mirrored panel, rolling over and over, laughing each time she met her own eyes. "I want to go again."

Adam stood silently in the middle, looking at the floor, counting the paint specks on the linoleum. "Give me those vials back, Donald."

A look of terror came over his face. "What? Why?"

"Party's over."

Cat tossed the joint on the floor and stamped it out. "Shit's got seeds in it. Whose was that?"

"It's mine," Bug said through gritted teeth.

A pause. "You should get some new some shit."

"You should get your *own* shit."

They tumbled through the basement corridors, past the faulty wires dangling from ceiling to floor, jumping about like a severed limb, leaping and sparking with ferocity.

The hailstones hit them hard as they exited out the fire escape. They all leapt over the gap between the roofs with ease, the sound of police sirens approaching like Ecstasy coming on.

Once beyond the River Oak grounds they rested at an out-of-service bus stop. Donald took his tweed hat off and looked at it in surprise. "Hey, I forgot I had this."

Adam downed something from one of the vials returned to him. "At least the night hasn't been a total waste of time, then."

He leaned on his knees and huffed, "I haven't ran so much since I got pinched by that bastard security guard at HMV."

Bug cradled Fiona, feeding her a cigarette like a nursing mother. Cat kept at a distance, arms folded tightly again, still whining about her notes and her Portishead CD all the way back to Paisley, leaving Bug and Fiona in Renfrew, saying they knew someone who was having a house party as their parents were away for a fortnight.

On Cat's street every driveway pillar had an identical silver plate with the house number on it, then a twenty-foot high double door, hiding the house behind it.

The first thing Donald had said in an hour was, "We should have stopped by Renfrew. I know a guy that sells crack."

Adam marched on. "Donald, how many times? We're not buying crack."

Cat stopped outside her house and flashed a fob over a secure entry system on the driveway pillar, opening up a view of the front lawn filled with pigeons and the house in total darkness. It was the emptiest looking house on the street.

"Your dad still not home" Adam asked gingerly.

"Nah. Berlin. Business. Again. Mum's extending her stay at Stobo Castle. 'Relaxing' she says."

"So is it a good story? How much, legally, can you say about any of this?"

"I don't know yet. Depends on what the lawyers say."

"Are they still gonna kill you off? The magazine?"

"I don't know. I think I can talk them round with an abortion or something lighter. Just an overdose or an alleged rape, maybe. That ought to stave them off for a few weeks." She stuck her chewing gum that she had only just opened, to the driveway pillar. "Thanks for looking after me." She pecked Adam on the cheek and ran up the driveway.

Donald started, "Are there any Renfrew buses around here…?"

Adam sighed, "Donald, please."

Chapter Eight
'The Scottish Play'

Awakening numb; braced for the pounding headache. Leftover pizza sat dried and curling up on a plate on the floor, the air muggy like stale summertime. Adam sat up with a groan and downed a Seroxat with a mouthful of warm lager and switched off the TV that had been playing all night. Due to the cold snap he had taken to wearing a thick jumper and woolly hat in bed. The wind whistled through the seal of the single-glazed window and he pulled the bed sheets up to his chin, listening to the next door neighbours already arguing. It was as if they opened their eyes in the morning then immediately started shouting from where they left off the night before, like their batteries had momentarily fallen out. Their noise was muffled but sustained; their dog started barking and downstairs a washing machine rumbled up through the floorboards and the rubbish lorry beeped outside on the main road – Adam's head ached in such a way as to make him adopt the foetal position, scrunching his woolly hat up off his head – and the radiators were clanging because of the vibrations and the postman chucked the mail through the door, letting the flap slam loudly, thoughtlessly, and Adam's nausea returned where it had left off and he took another Seroxat.

The front page of the freebie newspaper read, 'Mall Raid Ends in Terror!' The article continued for two further pages inside, '…last night saw a daring raid on the River Oak Shopping Centre to stop a gang of rampaging teenagers. Twelve were arrested at the scene but it is believed that at least four escaped capture. They are not thought to be armed or dangerous.'

Adam laughed so hard the lager came out his nose at the thought of the GOMA Kids being armed and dangerous. "The Stoner Provos. The Drunk-As-Fuck-Paras," he spluttered to himself, his laughter subsiding upon seeing his reflection in the mirrored wardrobe.

As soon as Adam opened the close door he was met with a blizzard and the wail of police sirens speeding past. He imperceptibly slumped against the wall. It was too early for such trauma.

Commuters and business people stormtrooped through Caledonia Street in their cars, just passing through to get to the motorway. Paisley was that sadly necessary, and savage, partition to where you really wanted to go; always just passing through. Feet twitched on the accelerator pedals, desperate to get through the traffic lights before Adam halted their progress.

A woman in a clapped out Mondeo slowed as the lights changed to amber, a BMW screeching to a halt behind her. He thrashed on his horn then, realising he needed to make a bigger statement, ran up to her car. He pounded on her window, yelling "You IDIOT! You could of got through then!"

Adam crossed to the other side, taking a break for his trembling legs by leaning on the railings. The man carried on screaming as the lights turned to green and the woman drove off – his car now blocked the entire road to a cacophony of car horns and revved engines. He stood there waving his fist in the air, seemingly oblivious to the snow soaking through his shirt, his face freezing bright red. "You fucking *bitch…*" He started to cry and struck his thighs repeatedly with his fists until someone attempted to help him back in his car.

Under Gilmour Street Bridge a homeless man sat where the snow hadn't yet drifted into, pigeons pecking about in the whitening puddles. His lips moved, and although he was inaudible Adam knew what he was saying: "Any spare change?" His words had become less and less clear with each day Adam passed him. The mist came out of his mouth, inanimate as a kettle, and he hugged himself tightly, looking into his Styrofoam cup on the ground every few seconds, hopelessly checking its pitiful contents, but still Adam didn't believe the man's harrowing obstinacy. Adam stood over him, staring dumbly at a poster for discounted beer above the man's head. "I...eh...I'm sorry. Mate." The last word rang out hollowly around the decaying, moss-coated walls. The man kept staring straight ahead, still mouthing away, not noticing Adam was even there.

A group of women in Burberry miniskirts huddled together, arms linked, bracing the snow, traipsing back home after late night parties, the sound of their heels clicking out under the bridge. None of them looked at Adam. One described her blowjob experience:

"Seerisly, Lynn, hen. In ma hair and evryfin. Whit wis a mentae do..." The girl pulled out the strands of bleached hair still stuck together with the guy's semen – freezing to a mould in the wintry air.

At the rows of bus stops, Paisley folk let their heads hang low, tucked into their jacket collars, standing still, dismally checking their watches to the sound of a Venezuelan pan pipe band dressed in ponchos playing across the street, seemingly at home in the snow.

"Do you know any Lonnie Donegan, son?" a passing pensioner wheezed.

His friend pulled him away. "They only do that Italian chicka-

chicka stuff, Archie, come on, leave them alone."

As the men shuffled away from their bus shelter, Adam noticed a tag, spray painted with 'The Eton Boys' in pristinely applied italics.

On campus, students were running around waving pieces of paper in the air, cursing madly. It was resit day – that last chance to pass. It was the same people every year: they spent all semester drinking and partying and getting laid in West End flats paid for by their parents.

"Where the fuck is the library?" a girl shouted in the square, oblivious that she was already standing in front of it.

Her friend cried, "I'm like, so stressed," then held up her John Lewis bags in defeat.

Adam made his way towards the English building and noticed, lurking in the dark alleys and passageways around the snow covered quadrangle, hidden away from the CCTV cameras, were strange figures. They were dressed in the same outfits as the two that had haunted Adam's Hugh MacDiarmid lecture. A boy asked out the corner of his mouth, looking away from the vendor. "You got Civil Engineering or Physics?" Money quickly changed hands along with one of the papers, and the boy walked off. The vendor hid under the brim of his bowler hat and said to another student, "I've got Politics and Economics for a tenner," then conspicuously waved a piece of paper down by his waist. The boy's bow tie sported a Hutchie Grammar logo.

Adam tried not to look at the transaction as he walked past.

"Oh come on, I don't have a tenner," the student said with a sense of overwhelming injustice. "Five."

"Peasant," the vendor grumbled.

Adam froze as soon as he heard it. "Eddie!" he growled.

Eddie looked up, incredulous for a second, then grabbed his money from the boy and ran away, his papers flying up and away in all directions in the scuffle. The Seroxat left Adam several steps behind, giving up on catching him before he had even made it round the corner of the library. He followed Eddie, rounding the building, walking straight into Alex, a fellow English Lit student, whose head was buried in a copy of Evelyn Waugh's Vile Bodies.

"Sorry, I didn't even see you there," he mumbled, not lifting his sight from the pages. He finally looked up. "Adam. I'm glad I've bumped into you-"

Adam scoured the crowd in front of the library, rising up on his tip toes. "The guy with the bowtie. Did you see him?"

"What guy? Look, you didn't buy any of those papers did you?"

"No, why?"

"They're fakes. They're all the wrong answers."

"Who are they? The sellers?"

Alex looked over his shoulder, like he was being followed, his long hair dishevelled in the wind. "I don't know, but I'm getting out of here. Class was cancelled."

"Cancelled? Bob never cancels."

He puffed, "He's cancelled today, let me tell you." He looked around the tops of the buildings like a paranoid informant. "There's police crawling all over the place. What a strange morning it's been." He flashed around like he'd seen something or someone out the corner of his eye and pulled Adam close by the collar. "I don't like it. I don't like it one bit. By the way, you got any uppers? I've got an exam to cram for."

"No, no, I've got nothing on me," he lied, pretending to feel around his pockets. "Why is class cancelled, Alex? What are the police doing here?"

"Everyone knows, Adam. It's old Arnott."

Adam held the lapel of his coat up to shelter the wind as he lit a cigarette. He exhaled, speaking through the smoke, "What about him?"

"He's popped his clogs."

"What?"

"Hung himself in the ole office, apparently. Shame. He hadn't given me my appraisal yet." He mumbled, "Such a strange morning…"

Adam ran off, the tails of his long tweed coat flapping around his legs.

Alex called out after him, "Hey wait, I need your notes for Cain's Book…"

A large crowd had gathered outside the front doors of the English building. It was cordoned off and several policeman stood behind the tape, hands behind their backs. A black van, that said 'Private Ambulance' on the side, trundled up with its lights on but no siren, and the medics got out slowly. They shared jokes on the way in: it was just another day.

Adam pushed slowly through the crowd to try to get to the front. An officer stepped out and blocked his path.

"Can I get through?" Adam asked. "I knew him, you see."

The officer shrugged, his hand kept ominously on his radio, wondering *Is this trouble?* His voice was a lot louder than necessary, to let everyone know who was in charge. "Sir, please step back from the tape. No one gets through."

Adam sat on a bench facing the building, watching the crowd slowly dissolve like the deconstruction of an acid trip. They had hoped to see the body being taken out. Adam stayed for a good half an hour until he saw someone he recognised. "Professor Bernstein?" he called out.

Bernstein had his arm around another lecturer. He straightened his canary yellow tie and held his matching pocket handkerchief to his mouth. Adam continued calling on him until he finally walked over.

"Professor Bernstein…"

"Oh Adam. My boy." Bernstein put his arm around Adam which he shrugged off quickly but delicately. "It's not best for you to be here just now."

Up at Bob's open office window his metal Venetian blinds were rattling in the wind, striking out at a lone pigeon flapping around on the ledge as if it was trying to get in.

Adam asked, "What does it look like up there?"

Bernstein looked up towards the window. "It's just very cold. He left the window open, I suppose." He blew his nose rigorously in his handkerchief then handed Adam a piece of paper from his inside jacket pocket. "I think maybe you should read that."

Adam held the note tightly as the front doors swung open. Through the crowd of policeman and medics, a black body bag on top of a stretcher was pushed out by two bored looking medics. Some lecturers from his department huddled around it, blocking Adam's view, then the back doors of the black van clattered shut, and Bob was gone.

Wheeled away like Fix It's damaged goods, Adam thought. "What is this? A suicide note?" he asked.

Bernstein nodded gravely. "Yes. Yes, I'm afraid it is."

The paper was expensive and folded crisply, the writing that of a skilled calligrapher. His plan had been well thought through. How long he had planned to do it Adam couldn't work out, but suddenly he felt a huge responsibility for all of it, after their argument – the last time he saw him.

Adam unfolded the note carefully and read the simple words: "'And it breaks my heart, to have to leave you here alone, trapped in The Scottish Play.'"

Professor Bernstein closed his eyes and said sagely, "The Scottish Play." He sighed. "He must have meant it for me."

Adam gulped hard. "Yeah. He must have."

He plucked the note from Adam's hand, its true recipient. "Thank you," Bernstein said and looked up at the sky. "I just think he would have wanted me to have this. Don't you?"

Adam shrugged at the futility of it all. "So, when do you think the funeral will be?"

Bernstein folded up the note and put it back in his pocket, then looked anxiously at the ground. "I shouldn't worry about that, Adam."

"Why is that?"

He cleared his throat. "I don't know how 'open' the funeral will be."

"Of course. That's only right."

At the front gates some first year students chased each other, running straight into Adam, as the blizzard started up again.

"Check it out, I'm the dead professor!" one said, throwing her cream winter coat over her head like a child pretending to be a Halloween ghost.

Adam ripped her jacket off and yelled, "Bob! His name was Bob, you parasites!"

George Square was deserted as the snow storm built in force, leaving only a few tourists taking photos of the statue of Sir Walter Scott. Adam took out the sandwiches he had made that morning, wrapped in cling film and cried, softly at first. Pigeons pecked around his feet where the filling was falling out his sandwiches. The pigeons swarmed, reacting with the same lack of feeling the humans had. "Oh…FUCK IT!" Adam screamed and kicked wildly at the birds – managing to hit a few – then he slipped in the snow and fell to the ground. Some of the tourists stared across at him, their cameras poised, unsure whether to snap him or not.

"What do you want?" Adam wiped himself down and yelled, "It's a tradition here, alright. In this country, we kick the pigeons."

On the way home he stopped at Haddows to buy some Totov vodka. The fluorescent strip light on the ceiling of the shop burned through his eyes like a newborn, trying to ignore the long queue, and the fact that everyone had lottery tickets in their hands.

When it came to Adam's turn, he dropped his bottles down on

the counter.

"Hello again," the clerk said.

"I'm just gonna put this on my credit card if that's alright..."

Once upstairs, Adam poured large, obscene measures of vodka into a tumbler, like it was water – measures even he knew he couldn't handle. By the afternoon he was slumped on the hall floor, reaching out against the door to the postman's footsteps echoing and then fading out as the close door shut behind him. The more he drank the further he tried to distance the thought – the truth – that he had failed Bob. Adam hadn't been sure upon arriving on campus whether or not he was going to continue on at Thistle; he knew the answer now. And he couldn't even cry about it. He wanted to so much.

The only other thing he could think of was to fetch the clippers from his wardrobe and started carving thick lands of hair from his scalp. Watching the hair fall away so easily comforted him, like wiping away dirt. His face started taking a different shape. He was new.

Chapter Ten
'Medicine and rest'

The doctor's surgery throbbed with bodies, their heads dangling atop chubby chins, mouths straight as dashes – they were always so stern, unhappy, these people, Adam thought, quietly burping downwards into his chest, the result of mixing drinks over breakfast. It was the first time he had heard a voice other than his own, or been in a room with anyone else, for over a week, except for wordless transactions at the off license, the teller packing his bags as scornfully as possible, trying to let Adam know how monstrous it was to be buying booze at such an early hour. He had taken to putting on a shirt and tie and an old blazer to buy his drink, in the hope that he would at least look moderately civilised, that he must be buying ahead of time for a classy party being dressed like that. He must have a respectable job... Every time Adam looked out the living room window of his flat – facing the frantic shoppers with their stripy carrier bags and ugly dogs – the streets seemed emptier than before. The spaces between the bodies was growing; in the surgery, everyone was locked together in the same struggle, eager to renew their prescriptions for nullifying meds, or to get another dubious sick line signed.

Adam sat amongst a seemingly endless sea of fat, red faces, all moaning about "the fucking NHS":

"I mind when I could get ma valium ayer the counter," a woman said, cradling a baby in one arm, a toddler in the other – both wailing in a fashion that suggested neither thought they were in the right woman's arms. She threw a toy down on the floor for the toddler then yanked out a flabby tit for the baby.

Adam slouched down in the front row, taking quick blasts of whisky from a hip flask as he read a women's Cosmopolitan magazine quiz ('I prioritise my career ahead of sex and a loving husband, according to this'). The receptionist called out his name and he tossed the magazine down on the seat adjacent with a loud slap.

On Doctor Hamsun's desk sat a flip pad calendar which read, '25th October' written in bold black letters. As Adam's mind slipped away the letters seemed to morph into '21st December'. What is this hallucination?, he giggled to himself, then concentrated more severely, shutting his eyes with a grimace. He saw a graveyard.

The walls of the surgery were safe and white; a spotlight hung over the examination bed, and posters of cartoon amoebas and toy parasites moulded in plasticine filled the walls. There were lights in every corner of the room, no space was unlit. Halogen spotlights, UVA lights, forty, sixty, one-hundred watts, all buzzing constantly in different semi-tones. A poster behind Hume's desk informed Adam that a third of the entire planet will contract some form of cancer in their lifetime. Lifetime, he thought. "What a strange phrase… lifetime."

The doctor rushed in and took a seat without looking at Adam, then rubbed his eyes while slowly arranging pieces of paper he pulled from a scuffed, brown briefcase. Without warning, he pulled Adam's castor-wheeled chair towards him and flashed his torch in his eyes. "Been doing some…drinking this morning?" he asked, straining with concentration.

Adam wiggled his hand. "A little."

Hume sat back and they looked at each other for a moment, then he pushed some papers along the desk which he told Adam to sign.

"Are they important?" Adam asked.

"Nope."

Hume was a puffy, rusty octogenarian that spoke in a curt Scottish accent. Thick wads of hair crept out his ears like ivy, tangling in the arms of his glasses.

"So," he started, keeping eyes down whilst highlighting sentences on the papers Adam had just signed. "How are *things*?"

"*Things*? Not great, doc. I've been having trouble sleeping. The Percocet and the Lustral don't seem to be working anymore. Maybe if you increase the dosage…"

He didn't think twice, but if he had looked up he would have seen Adam's cheeky monkey smirk. It really was all too easy. "More Paxil, as well then," he said and scribbled down the prescription. "The Percocet is what's giving you that jaundice complexion. By god, you're practically yellow. I want you to start eating more too, your cheekbones are jutting out. Like looking at a damn coathanger. And we'll have to do something about those brown rings around your eyes."

"Yes, unfortunately I've been drinking quite a lot to get to sleep."

"Some more Seroxat will put a stop to that."

Adam tapped his foot reassuringly. "Yep, that's what I thought. Cos that stuff's got quite a kick with a few shots of whisky in the morning." It also had quite a kickback selling at £10 a pop to the GOMA Kids.

Hume wasn't listening. "Now, just sign this here and I can get

97

back to work."

Adam signed the prescription.

"I have to ask you, on your record it mentions the 21st December with regards to counselling last year."

Adam reached across and flipped through Hume's calendar. "What is that? Is that St Andrew's Day? I always forget…"

Hume examined his counselling record. "Says here you suffered a bereavement then. 1992?"

Adam looked at him in puzzlement, his smirk long gone. "It doesn't matter, it was a long time ago. Nothing good old medicine can't take care of," he mumbled, his enthusiasm broken.

"Winter blues. That's all. Whatever's wrong with you…" He scribbled down something. "…it'll pass. Medicine and rest." He leaned into him and sniffed. "You've been smoking this morning. Do you know what that stuff does to your insides?" He tossed a cancer leaflet at him. The front cover was a cigarette with a cartoon/human face wagging his white-gloved finger. The speech bubble read: 'Do you know how many people a year die from smoking?'

Adam sat back in complete acceptance as Hume readied his golf bag next to the examination table. "I know," Adam said, "I'm going to end up with cancer. Every little puff rots my insides black. Hell, just sign me up for chemo just now. I take it there's a waiting list." The morning of drink and pills had totally twisted him, and now he just wanted to get out of there so he could continue. "If you don't mind I've a funeral to go to."

"Here's your prescription." Hume handed Adam the yellow slip, walking ahead of him out the door, golf bag over his shoulder.

Adam looked down at the enormous amounts he had written down, accidentally giving him a good four months' worth. But still he felt brave, pursuing Hume through the reception area:

"How do you expect me to survive on this? Little crackhead babies in Renfrew couldn't last on this shit. Hey, come back here…I suppose a lollipop is out of the question?"

Hume threw the doors open, calling back over his shoulder, "Only if you caddy me."

"You demon!" Adam laughed manically at the mammoth haul he had tweezed out him.

The receptionist, painting her nails, jumped as Adam slammed Hume's door behind him, spilling her red varnish over patient's files.

Adam leaned over the desk, mopping some of the varnish with his finger, methodically wiping a red stripe across each cheek from the bridge of his nose. The receptionist recoiled. "I don't suppose you know where I can find a good black tie?"

Chapter Eleven

‘   ’

The hearse pulled up outside the church, family and friends holding on to each other as the rain poured down in fat greasy drops like chip pan oil.

Adam looked on, hanging through the iron railings like a jailbird, dressed in a black suit and tie (Cancer Research Shop – 50p) smoking a cigarette, the red stripes streaking down his face in the rain. Each time he looked at the cigarette tip, he saw the cartoon-man from Hume's wagging his finger at him. He took out his flask of whisky from his inside pocket and took a long drink. It was about a hundred yards to the church entrance; he could have walked in, taking a seat near the front rows if he wanted, but it made more sense to stay back, out of the crowd, observing alone, exiled, as he did in his flat; solitude was becoming an absolute, his way of life, how he *lived*. He wasn't capable of providing company or solace; he was becoming as inanimate as a telescope, only as useful as they things he was pointed at.

Professor Bernstein loomed large amongst the other University lecturers – impeccable suit as always: a surprisingly understated black two piece. He held a black handkerchief with pink polka dots on it, wiping his eyes as he cried, almost too hysterically, like he was trying to prove his grief. An old man – Bob's father - with a cane shuffled along slowly at the front – he looked scared, like he didn't understand what was happening, lost in a glade of senility. A younger woman pushed him through the front door, into a darkness.

The procession made its way inside, not noticing the smattering of people looking on outside the gates.

"That wuman's dress is gorgeous innit?"

"Aye. That's BHS in all."

"Naw!"

"Aye. You can get a crackin' dress in there for aboot twenty quid…"

One of them looked at Adam swigging. "You awright, son? The polis'll nick you if they see you with that." She shuddered when she noticed his makeup.

He offered them a drink but they walked off towards the city centre with their extra-strong fabric shopping bags. The coffin disappeared inside and the main doors closed slowly, and firmly, behind, sucking up the vacuum of grief now locked inside. A dirty pigeon swooped down with tattered wings on to a wooden sign beside the door that read, 'God is my father and my shepherd.'

"Some shepherd," Adam mumbled.

He slouched in front of the news with a bottle of cheap red wine. It tasted almost rancid as he had to push the cork down into the bottle; he drank it anyway, forgoing another meal. The afternoon ran away quickly yet he felt no difference in his state, no matter how much I drank. Drunk, yes, chemically altered, yes, but no change in actual feeling.

He was just about to pass out when the phone rang, wrenching him out of his slump. He only lifted the receiver to stop the noise, but as he was about to drop the phone back down in its cradle, he heard – through throbbing tinnitus – "Adam? It's Lucy."

"Lucy. Lucy." He contemplated her name like it had been years.

"How are you, bruv? You sound <u>drunk</u>."

"I feel...very happy."

"You're not drinking alone again are you?"

"No, course not. Em...Gerald is here," he said, shrugging his shoulder to himself at who Gerald was supposed to be. "He's a bit shy, though, aren't you?" he said to no one.

"Well, tell him I said, hi."

A pause.

"So have you seen Dad recently?" she asked.

He coughed violently. "Yeah, I...well, not really. No. He's been calling looking for money."

"Mm. Me too. Was he drunk?"

"Yeah, steaming. He's getting worse, I think. Look, I need to go I'm just meeting a friend."

Another pause. "I thought you had someone up already?"

"Oh, I do. He's...eh...coming with me."

"Maybe we should meet for lunch or something. I don't know. We should just talk."

"How..." He panicked, "I mean, *when*. I meant to say when." He felt tears forming.

The pause was heavier in the air this time. "Are you alright? You can tell me if something's wrong."

Somehow Adam managed to cough the tears back down: years of practicing illusion. "Oh, look just call me, OK?" he whimpered.

"I am. I'm calling you now. Why don't you want to talk? Do you know how long it's been?"

He thought about it then answered honestly. "I really couldn't say." His foot knocked over the lightbox sitting in front of him.

"What's that noise?"

"Don't worry about it. It's just some old drunk." He walked to the window to survey the street below: The last of the sun fell below the horizon, surrendering to its inescapable cycle. How tragic, Adam thought, to be the sun. No escape, no life: just attendance. The sickly blue light from the tanning salon beamed out onto the street whenever a cubicle door opened, their ersatz sun; it was what Adam imagined cancer looked like, sitting by his mother's dressing table, his legs flapping in the air, watching her squirm on her bed as it worked its way through her bloodstream. Some of the salon customers were waiting outside for a fag break before going back in for another hit of the light. A drunk was screaming at them to the tune of 'War is Over': "A merry FUCKING Christmas…and a Happy New Year!"

"It's a bit early for that, Granddad," one of the tanners responded.

All along the street people hung out their windows, shouting at the drunk. There hadn't been so many people hanging out windows since Wall Street in 1929.

The tanning party stubbed out their fags, and moved back inside to the blue light, where it felt safe.

Smoke rose like molehills across the dusk light, the sun looking on, stuck, as the cosmos continued to grow with every second, further and further away from Adam and the sun, at a rate of sixteen thousand miles a day.

Lucy beckoned, "…Adam, Adam, are you still there."

"Even the stars want to get away from all this," Adam said, his head resting against the cold glass of the window.

"What do you mean?"

"The sun is lonely. I can tell."

"Look, I'm coming back into town in a few weeks to lay some flowers at the cemetery…" She was struggling to be heard now, as a feral dog of hers barked away at her feet. She was tap dancing around it, the phone line wrapping itself around her ankles.

Maintaining conversation – however brief – in his condition had been exhausting, and he was now desperate to resume his rest. As Lucy continued talking – updating him on what family members were no longer talking to him now because of all the birthdays he had forgotten – the bag of weed on the coffee table came into focus, ever clearer; reality was starting to invade his head again; it was time to pull the plug.

"Lucy, I've got to go," he said sounding suddenly harassed by domesticity. All he could think about now was getting the joint made and smoking it. Nothing else in life mattered until that happened. "I've got some food in the oven."

He hung up and rolled the joint as fast as he could, dropping the papers he was in such desperation for the hit, angry tears flowing in a rage at his clumsiness. When he took a drag he managed to forget a little more. He fell asleep on the sofa for the fourth night in a row, dreaming about Bob and fathers: one was in the sky, one was on the TV, one was in Downing Street, one was in Berlin on business, and one was in the pub playing slot machines with his benefit money.

105

Chapter Twelve

'Mike Leigh Season'

Litter flew up and around – as if controlled by string – the open doors of the Glasgow Film Theatre. Showing, presently, was a preview of 'Nil By Mouth', part of the Mike Leigh Season. There was no queue for tickets – there never was at that time of the morning – just several lonely looking students (a collection of cardigans and side partings) scouring the pages of the cinema guide (free if you see more than seven films a week) and some tourists asking if 'The English Patient' was still playing. The loners had an unspoken etiquette, like old men's rules about when to take your jacket off at the bowling club.

The girl at the ticket booth was a heavy set. She's got a bit of the Goth, a bit of the puff pastry about her, Adam thought. She had applied a thick flash of black eyeliner that looked like a mistake, and thick pale foundation caked on around her cheeks and chin, which failed to hide her pimples that peeked the makeup like Braille. Her name badge said, 'Laura'.

"One. *Nil By Mouth* at ten, please," Adam mumbled.

"Huh?" she shouted abrasively through the glass window – her tone suggested a weariness of talking to shy loners all morning. "It starts in five minutes, you know." She brushed his finger as she passed the ticket through.

Adam blushed deep red then tripped on the edge of the carpet as he walked away. The others standing around all thought the same thing: "glad that wasn't me."

The regulars had scattered to all corners of the small cinema, each in their own favourite space, most of them avoiding the centre, where they were liable to have to sit within a close proximity to someone else. All they wanted was room, space to be alone. The bright house lights were still to dim – so harsh Adam could sense the discomfort in the room – as he entered. It was silent except for the occasional awkward fumbling with sweet packets that was followed by a mumbled 'sorry'. The room was so cold Adam could see his breath hanging in the air. He folded his arms and hugged himself tightly.

Across the aisle from, a man dressed completely in green corduroy and wearing pince-nez caught Adam drinking from his flask. He sheepishly offered him a drink. Green corduroy blinked and looked back at the blank screen in disgust, then checked his watch as if to emphasise how early it was.

Adam shrugged. "Suit yourself."

The others shifted uncomfortably in their seats; they sensed Adam was trouble.

The girl from the ticket booth stood in the entryway at the side of the seat gallery, looking around. Adam had nowhere to go and only one direction to look in. He felt her staring directly at him, so he shuffled around in his bag in a panic, pretending to look for something, then finally relief, as the lights came down and the adverts started.

The screen flickered white for a few seconds as he took another drink, just long enough for Laura to notice the raising and falling motion of his arm, the glint of the silver. He put the flask back in his bag and slouched down, peeking over the seat in front. She was walking towards him.

Oh shit, Adam thought, *I'm barred for sure.*

She leaned in and whispered, "You gonna give me a drink of that, or what?" and took a seat next to him.

The man with the pince-nez shushed her.

She sat closest to the aisle, which Adam immediately knew was trouble. He was trapped.

She held out her hand and said, "Laura."

"Adam." Her grip was a lot stronger than his, and thought nothing of pushing his elbow over in order to get the arm rest.

Several minutes of the film passed before either of them said anything further; her hand crept slowly over the arm rest on to his lap.

"Don't you have to work?" he whispered.

"I am. I'm making sure no one's recording the film."

"You could just pop your head in once in a while, though." Adam cursed his growing penis making an escape impossible.

As the movie continued she started running her hand up and down his leg making him flinch and judder, her long fingernails catching in the weave of his trousers. She leaned in close to him, trying to whisper seductively whilst still chewing gum.

She has a funny smell about her, Adam thought.

During a scene of frenetic violence and swearing she chose to lunge in and rammed her piston tongue into his mouth. She had a strange stale taste – like a hospital floor. She rolled her tongue around and around his mouth, her chewing gum bouncing off his tongue every so often. Adam sat there impassively until she stopped.

He nodded towards the screen. "That was a nice edit, there, d'you see that."

"Want to get out of here?"

Adam nodded, mouth hanging open, too scared at the repercussions of doing otherwise.

"So where do you stay?" she asked leading him outside, spitting her gum out with a *pwhoft*.

Adam stammered, "Um…um Paisley." He could barely keep up with her, and he kept looking over his shoulder, expecting someone to help, like the police or a priest with experience in exorcisms.

She groaned, "Paisley, huh? *Shit*. Do you live yourself?"

"Uh huh."

"I can drive us there. Just give me directions once we're close."

They were hurtling down the motorway in a tin can of a Vauxhall Nova, the stereo blaring 'Shook Me All Night Long' by AC/DC with the windows down. At over 80mph it didn't seem like the car could handle it, breaking up upon re-entry like the Columbia space shuttle. Everything rattled or shook; the car was filled with all sorts of litter, crisp packets, chocolate wrappers (neither necessarily empty), cans of coke. Not to say that she was *grossly* overweight, but in the car Adam felt like a toothpick in comparison – something she wasn't afraid to point out.

"Someone should put you in one of those adverts. How about 'save the starving people of Paisley' and shit…"

She pulled up at his building, tyres screeching, nearly ramming the bottom floor flats as she parked like a drunken rally driver. As they ran upstairs – her in desire for her lay, Adam in desire to just get it over with – she had already started pulling both their clothes off.

"How many fucking floors up are you?" she asked, running out of breath.

"Three." His heart was pounding as she ruffled through his chest of drawers. This wasn't how he saw himself losing his virginity.

"Where's your condoms, Alan?"

"Adam."

"What? Never mind, I've got some. It's supposed to be the guy's thing but whatever…"

Adam didn't know where to look as she undressed down to her ill-fitting black thong and pink bra.

"It's fucking freezing in here. You done this before?"

"Sure…I…"

"Good," she said and lunged at him, knocking over the lightbox on the bedside cabinet. She pushed him down on to the freezing cold carpet and whacked a condom on him. He cried out in agony.

"Ooh, you like that don't you, bitch," she said.

"No, honestly…"

She climbed on top and sighed a deep, "Oh yeah!", as his pelvis disappeared inside her black hole (nothing survives)… A golden crucifix dangled from her neck, right in front of his face. He tried not to look at it, but she just kept rolling around on top of him, digging her fingers deep into his back and the crucifix was hitting him in the forehead with every grating, wet thrust.

She cried out, "Oh Alan, Alan!" and moaned and groaned intermittently.

Adam's erection faded the more he looked at her.

She said gruffly, "Hurt me."

"What?"

"Hurt me."

"You…you want me to hurt you?"

"Yes! Yes!"

Oh Christ, he thought. She's one those chicks that's 'into' asphyxiation and shit like that. He kept saying in quiet disbelief to himself, "You don't even know me, you don't even know me…"

So he climbed on top of her (it took a while, and the same effort it takes to perform several press-ups) and started nibbling at her pork-fat shoulder.

"No! Harder for fuck's sake!" she instructed.

The downstairs neighbour banged on his ceiling for them to "keep the fucking noise down. Fucking kids. No fucking respect…"

She lunged at his chest, gnarling at it like a hungry dog and said almost breathlessly, "Are you close, are you close? I'm really close," then rubbed her hand over his shaved head.

Adam wasn't entirely sure what she meant by "close."

"Ooh baby, I love your fucking shaved head." Then out of nowhere she asked, "Do you believe in God?"

"What?"

Her face curled up and she grabbed the side of his head. She rattled it up and down and screamed, "DO YOU BELIEVE IN GOD? CALL ME THE VIRGIN MARY! CALL ME THE FUCKING VIRGIN MARY! I'M THE VIRGIN MARY! MAKE ME PURE!"

Adam was too scared to think of anything to say. "Do you want me to?"

She goaded him on and muttered things to her self. He looked down at her eager face, so desperate to be someone's object that he felt like sobbing. Every movement she made revealed another imperfection, another blemish on her body: her legs were patchy with hair where she had been waxing crudely and messily, and her stretch marks pulsed in and out of their pink crevices with every thrust. The rolls of her stomach overlapped and crashed into each other like duelling tidal waves. The only thing Adam could do was shut his eyes and try to ignore it, as if he had left the television on at a high volume with no way of turning it off – his legs started to tremble and an orgasm eked its way up from the pit of his stomach.

Laura groaned heavily again and put the crucifix in her mouth, biting down on it.

Adam came weakly and she collapsed across his bloody chest.

"That was…fucking…brilliant, Alan," she sighed.

"That was…new," he replied and carefully removed her arm from his body.

"Sorry about the Virgin Mary thing. It's just been a fantasy of mine. You looked like one of those wierdos that wouldn't mind. No offence…"

"No, none taken."

What do people say after sex? Will she know I'm a rank amateur?

"That was the best sex I've had in ages," Adam announced. *There, that'll fool her. I'm so clever.*

She moved her left leg up and down the inside of his thigh, her stubble scraping his skin, her sweat warm and sticky like Sunday-lunch gravy. Adam jumped up and ran to the bathroom, his hamstrings trembling. This was just a horrible mistake, he explained to the mirror. A moment of weakness.

Laura shouted, "Hey, you got any food? Fucking really gets my appetite going…"

Adam got down on his knees and ran the taps as loud as possible to cover up his vomiting. When he came back into the bedroom she was hurriedly putting her clothes on.

"Hey, what's the matter?" he asked, still naked in front of her. "You heard me throwing up, right…"

She put on her black biker boots.

"Look it's not you, I just drank a bit too much last night…"

She stepped back away from him. "You are so full of shit, you know that!" she yelled then stormed out to the hall.

Adam leaned against the door, cupping himself (sensing that something might be thrown at him). "Right, what the fuck is going on here? Right, OK. You got me, I'm a virgin. There I said it. Was I really that bad? You came didn't you? Your chest and face was all red. I know what that means, I read about it in 'American Psycho' when Patrick Bateman shags that model-"

She didn't seem to notice this confession. "What is this fucking shit?" She was hysterically waving a copy of 'Why I Am Not A Christian' by Bertrand Russell in his face. "Are you an atheist or something?"

Adam shrugged. "More of an anti-theist. You see I don't even like the idea of a-"

She cut him off, "You're such a degenerate. I thought you were a nice Christian boy as well..."

She was still doing up her bra on the way down the stairs.

For some absurd reason it made Adam think of 'A Whole Lot of Rosie' by AC/DC: the most inappropriate song to think of at that moment. He picked up the Bertrand Russell book and scrambled to the living room, throwing the curtains, then the window wide open.

He shouted down to her, "Hey Laura, judge not lest ye be judged, you fucking slapper!"

She looked up and gave him the finger.

It was such a basic, yet profound, insult. He paused then screamed back at the top of his lungs, "Well, *fuck* you too!"

Some women gathered down by the Tanning Salon looked up at him, pointing, horrified at his skinny, naked, mutilated body.

Then just before she got in her car Adam screamed out, "And my name isn't fucking, ALAN! FUCK, I CAN'T BELIEVE I JUST LOST MY VIRGINITY TO YOU, YOU FUCKING TRAMP! THAT DIDN'T OFFICIALLY COUNT. I AM DECLARING A VIRIGINITY ANNULMENT!" The women were still looking up at the window in amazement as he slammed the window shut, almost taking it off its hinges. "FUCK!" he screamed at the ceiling and sat down on the floor to compose himself.

He ripped open a bottle of wine he hadn't planned on having until at least lunchtime. He spat out the cork and took a few chugs and reached for the phone.

A girl with a delicate voice picked up. "Hello, Glasgow Film Theatre, how can I help?"

In the calmest most composed voice possible, he said, "Hello there, can you tell me if you will be showing *Nil By Mouth* again tomorrow?"

Chapter Thirteen
'Halloween'

Some GOMA Kids gathered outside their usual spot dressed up in black PVC outfits, wool hair pieces and carrying pumpkins. Adam sat and observed them, waiting for the lights to come on above the Gallery. The council had erected string netting, webbed from roof to roof on the surrounding buildings, stretching across the whole square – primarily to stop the pigeons flying around – with thousands of tiny white fairy lights attached to it, a desperate attempt to fake a starry sky. The real ones were obscured by the thousands of streetlights beaming up thoughtlessly to the night sky.

Adam checked his watch then spoke to the lights. "You're late tonight."

Some GOMA Kids sat on the steps, lifting up their sleeves, comparing scars.

"I did *this* one last week, and *this* one yesterday," a girl in a Placebo T-shirt mumbled.

Her friend weighed in, "No, look here, these are way deeper than yours."

They held their arms side by side as the group huddled round to decide: the democracy of mutilation.

Another girl sat on the steps by herself, oblivious to any Halloween merriment. Her thumbs were wrenched through small holes at the bottom, keeping the sleeves down at all times. She sat close enough to the others to suggest that she had arrived with them but throughout the night she had somehow drifted – or the others had drifted – away.

117

A mother drove up in her Mercedes 4x4 beside the crowd on the pavement and rolled down her window. "Jane. Jane, honey. Ready when you are!"

The Placebo girl pulled her sleeve back down and huffed, "Oh god, it's my bitch mum. I wish she was dead."

Her friend snorted, "Yeah, totally."

"Ye-ah! Totally!"

Adam glanced away quickly.

The other parents arrived, forming a queue like a taxi rank, to equal derision from their kids as they stuffed themselves into the leather interiors: "I never *wanted* us to get this BMW…I hated that holiday in Florida, all that fucking sunshine…"

The sad girl was left on the steps. Thinking she was alone she put her head in her hands, then heard the murmurs of tourists and the clicking of cameras pointing up at the sky, which was suddenly aglow with the brightest, most tender light; the sky had cleared and there was nothing to be afraid of anymore. Adam looked up, noticing the star lights had now come on, filling the sky with thousands of glittering, tiny white specks. He smoked a cigarette, noticing the girl's disappointment, that it wasn't real. Just watching her. Admiring her strength. Her beauty in solitude.

The Pillbox was an old warehouse building, standing alone in a derelict industrial estate across from Dalmarnock train station. The neighbourhood was deserted at night, and no one knew about it except kerb crawlers and members of the police drug squad who would bust GOMA Kids occasionally for minor offences: various pills, illegal

Eastern European alcohol laced with Zandrupil; nothing out of the ordinary. The club inside was always filthy, tools left lying around in various states of disrepair. There were still fallen steel girders from industrial accidents, and broken lathes sitting orphaned in the car park, abandoned since the factory's final days. The owners had done practically nothing to it since opening it as a club, except install a PA system powered by a motor in the outside toilets; a bar was erected across an old iron work station; and the toilets were plumbed through in such a haphazard manner it was best to avoid standing under any dripping pipes.

It seemed as if everyone had dressed up much more elaborately than Adam: their faces were painted white, dressed like the dead for an open-casket funeral service, with large Robert Smith-eyeliner rings. Most of them had poorly applied red lipstick – a fashion some GOMA Kids were trying to start after watching Diane Ladd in 'Wild at Heart' – to look like blood, as if they had been sucking on virgin's necks all night. Everywhere there were ghouls running around.

Inside, the sound of 'Don't Fear the Reaper' built in volume as Adam trudged up the metal grate stairs winding up the side of the building, rain dripping through the holes in the flights above. The dance floor was filled with people swaying back and forth arrhythmically, completely out of time with the music, tripping on all sorts of pills, ridiculous coned joints dangling from their mouths, too out of it to manage lighting them. Donald stood at the sidelines dressed in a school uniform and shorts like Angus Young waiting for an AC/DC song to come on.

Adam headed straight for the bar, brandishing the fruits of three

119

Seroxat he had sold to the sad girl earlier at the Gallery. The bar was heaving, and Adam was unfortunately declined his request for a whole bottle of vodka. "Just give me two doubles then, I guess."

Nobody spoke, nobody really danced. In fact, no one did much of anything except constantly reapply their black eyeliner or kiss a stranger with a bored look on their face, mouth and eyes wide open, yawning into each other.

Security consisted of three skinheads, all in various punk bands that used the warehouse as a practice facility during the day. It didn't take much for them strong-arm the underagers. An aspiring GOMA Kid was hauled past Adam, protesting, "Hey, take it easy, man. I have depression, you know…"

Nicola stood by what passed for the cloakroom. She was wearing a black corset top with gold trim, ripped stockings and a thin flash of black eyeliner. Adam downed his drinks and approached with drunken restraint. The cinema had no further showings of 'Nil By Mouth' which had prompted some kind of panicked frenzy in him, that he would never get back that purity he had been so keen to get rid of. Now all he could think about was how much he wanted it back. The whole episode reminded him of his first glimpse of pornography back in primary school. The horror that there was hair down there between the woman's legs – sparse as it was – but it was the pinkness of the women's labia that had invaded his mind, how little it looked like what he thought it would. It was all so messy, hanging out there like that. How to get that innocence back? was the line that kept streaming through his mind, in a bright spectrum of light, like the time travel scene in '2001: A Space Odyssey'.

"Hey, Papillon," Nicola said pulling at Adam's black and white horizontal-striped shirt, then rubbed his head. "The streamlined look." She patted him on the cheek with a lazy smile. She had clearly been drinking before coming out too.

Adam swiped a glass of whisky someone had been stupid enough to leave unattended, and tossed it down his neck, taking an ice cube as he swallowed. He pointed at her with the empty cup. "You look a total mess."

"Thanks, so do you."

Adam pursed his lips together. "Thanks. Who are you supposed to be?"

"I was going to go as Madonna but I left my boob cones on the bus on the way here; my Mum thought I was a hooker."

She led Adam through a red curtain where there were sofas and tables bought from charity shops, or picked up from rubbish tips. Bug and Fiona lay draped across one of the hole-ridden sofas as if they had been there for hours. Candles were lit all around them – in fact, hardly a surface wasn't covered by a candle; the lighting had been deemed unsafe due to the leaking roof above.

Nicola led them to a table and chairs.

Adam asked the question that was impossible to convey casualness, "Aren't we going to wait for your boyfriend?"

She fluffed her hair up from the back. "He's just coming. We were away seeing the 'Jesus and the Paedos' gig across town."

"Oh yeah, was it any good?"

"Fucking shite."

"Cool."

The curtain flew back and in walked Cat, Cherry, Dick, Lucy, Tom, Harry, and Nicholas (with shaved head from his 'cancer'). They took the only sofa left, next to Adam and Nicola. Cat ignored Bug and Fiona then spotted their table. "Ohmygod, Adam, what are you doing here?" Then she noticed Nicola and moved in front of her. She was wearing a bizarre, wide brimmed hat, a long frumpy brown skirt and her hair was tied up in a loose bun, kept together with what looked like a pencil, and she had some strange prosthetic nose attached to her face.

Cat said quietly, "The magazine is dropping the whole killing-me-off thing."

"Oh yeah?" Adam droned, cursing inside that there was no bar nearby. "That's good."

"Yeah, they're going for the abortion instead. A happy compromise, they said. Which is, you know, *cool*."

Adam let out a blast of laughter, then quickly covered his mouth. He thought carefully before speaking. "Cat…you are going to be so… *famous*."

The others looked annoyed at having to get dressed up, probably at Cat's behest. Tom sat stony faced with a pair of plastic devil's horns and red cape.

Harry, dressed like Charlie Chaplin, said, "Don't they sell cigars in here? Where are the fucking waiters…"

Dick was dressed as Michael Jackson. He complained, "Don't they have any Danish house music, or Japanese space-punk? What kind of hovel is this…I told you we should have gone to the Art School, I couldn't gotten us passes…"

Nicholas was dressed like a hospital patient, with bandages on his wrists.

"Nice outfits, guys!" Adam said to them.

Dick smiled sarcastically. "Ha ha. We're here for the irony."

Tom said, "Yes, we're here for the irony."

Harry added, "Yes. The irony."

Cat waved at someone who clearly didn't recognise her. "Do you like my outfit, Adam?"

He nodded enthusiastically. "Yeah, definitely. That's really good…eh, who are you supposed to be?"

She rolled her eyes. "I'm Virginia Woolf. I like *your* costume too, Adam. It's lucky, that Auschwitz look is <u>so</u> in right now – you look that cool fucked up anorexic way. I'd definitely fuck you if I was fucked up."

Adam paused, wondering whether he should be worried.

She hurried to reassure him, laying her hand on his forearm. "No, that's good!" She went to the bar and bought back three trays' worth of booze.

A few yards away sat Bug and Fiona – she was spread-eagled across the sofa (to Bug's visible discomfort), wearing a black satin nightee (see-through) with plastic fangs hanging from her teeth, and her eyes rolling about in her head. She shifted position, falling into Bug's chest; he sat with his arm around her, two plastic bolts stuck on either side of his face which was painted green. Their bodies fitted together perfectly, causing Adam to see them blinking like Tetris shapes, as if they completed a line.

Bug caught sight of Adam and staggered over, blind drunk, and slapped him on the back. "Nice haircut."

"Hey, Frankenstein," Adam remarked. "How the *hell* did you two get in here?"

"Don't make me laugh. Hey, we should party tonight."

"Maybe later. Anyway, I can't take you seriously with that green face right now."

"Come on. It's our way of saying thanks for the Mall. I mean, we all know you only did it to get Cat out, but still, we owe you…" He slurped from his Bloody Mary and looked disappointed by Adam's reluctance. Fiona pulled him back on to the sofa by his shirt tails and kissed him, but as he opened his mouth he started to choke. "Honey, fangs; honey, *fangs!*" She took them out and they continued kissing.

Suddenly a hand landed on Adam's shoulder. He was no more than eighteen, and dressed like Mel Gibson in Braveheart, except for a black kilt, and his face was painted in a black Saltire.

Nicola stood up and pecked him on the cheek. "Adam, this is Trent."

"It's nice to meet you, Adam," he said.

Adam didn't know where to look. She had even left a trace of lipstick on Trent's cheek. Adam huffed, "So you're here to make my night fucking complete, right?"

Trent leaned in, raising his voice over the music which was playing painfully loud. "What?"

"I said, it's nice to finally meet you."

They shook hands.

I don't need this, Adam thought, eating into valuable drinking time. "Look, I don't have anything on me except for personal, so don't waste your time," Adam said, noticing his breath hanging in the air. A pause followed.

Trent poured himself a drink from the bottle of vodka he was holding then offered it to Adam, tossing the bottle top playfully at Bug and Fiona who were now sleeping. Trent patted Adam on the back, who reflexively flinched. Trent raised his glass and said, "Here's to good times."

Adam forced a smile, watching Nicola's hand creeping slowly into Trent's, his grip growing stronger, and then she fell into him totally, resting her head on his collar. Adam swallowed his drink in five bird-like mouthfuls which were the hardest work he had done all day. He got up – knees trembling as if he had just run a mile at a sprint – and grumbled, "Excuse me, excuse me" at everyone who got within a metre of him, stuffing pills into his mouth, until he reached the bar. The entire day had been too much to handle. He could still feel Laura in his hips, her temperature. He shook his head violently to dust off the memory, and kept looking down now, petrified of looking someone, anyone, directly in the eye – there was no telling what stories he would be told if he did so: all those Kids, in such a rush to get to the end, dancing like it was the last song of the century, drinking like the sun was about to evaporate everything, kissing like love was about to disappear, crying in the toilets like sadness was about to overcome everything, screaming like they had just realised how far away the next living creatures were in the universe, so far no one could be sure that the Earth wasn't intolerably alone, left to drift through the cosmos as punishment for god's own laziness. Adam began speaking these thought aloud at the bar, not to anyone in particularly: "…and so if

125

god doesn't help us, then he's either useless, or he doesn't care." He turned to the person to his left. "And what good is either outcome? I ask you!" His eyes were wide with fever now (or was it fervour? he didn't know the difference) believing he had latched on to some new truth. The blood was racing around his veins faster, his eyes were quicker to pick things up, the barman kept shovelling drinks out from under the bar, which Adam dutifully whisked back as quickly as they came. Then BANG. Everything stopped. The record slowed to a halt and Adam couldn't hear anything; ground zero. He closed his eyes as others continued to haunt his presence, but they couldn't he heard although their mouths were flapping. People were dancing courageously, grabbing each other, twisting, writhing around. Adam turned to each side, his head bobbing in slow motion, meeting the hollow eyes of a girl to his right who had been standing there listening to him jabber for the past twenty minutes. She took his hand.

It still felt like slow motion as she led him to the toilets, where the other girls smiled at them cheekily, and then the cubicle door was closed. Adam wasn't speaking anymore, instead concentrating on the reasons for why his trousers were down around his ankles now, why she was trying to grab hold of him, and he was inside her now and he didn't remember putting on a condom. All he could see was space, travelling through it, and then, the sound and normality returned. The volume went from zero to ten, and he felt the girl's sweat on his neck all of a sudden, her legs were definitely wrapped around his. She climbed off him and said, "So what's your name?"

Adam paused for a second, instinctively pulling his trousers back up, then he said, very carefully, "I'll tell you mine as long as you don't tell me yours."

She laughed as she closed the cubicle door behind her, just as it was reopened by Nicola, who for a second considered if she had gone through the wrong door.

Adam was still doing up his belt and flies, considering what to say. What came out was, "It's alright, Nicola, I don't love her."

Trent was still where Adam had left them, nearly an hour ago, toying with each other, and with Bug and Fiona who had now woken up. Especially Fiona, who had powder residue under her nostrils – perhaps a fleeting attempt to waken herself up. Adam rejoined them, sitting back down carefully, legs clamped together, still miles away, audio and visual coming in and out of operation, trying to digest the events of the last few minutes.

"So, Young Adam," Trent started with a mocking laugh, the bottle of vodka hanging from his fingertips between his legs which were wrenched far apart, "what do you do with yourself?"

Adam took a long time to lift his head up to Trent's line of sight, slowly opening his eyes. "Oh, just casual alcoholism, petty theft – when the opportunity presents itself - minor prescription drug dealing, watching the news."

"I hear you're working at Fix-It. I know a dealer in there called Mark. Good mate so he is. You know him?"

"Sure."

"Thieving little shite, so he is," he laughed. "And who are you with tonight?"

Adam shuffled in his seat, aware he was being mocked. He

127

couldn't even think of a name to make up for the girl that had just left him in the female toilets. "I…am with…god tonight. And he is with me. He's a terrible companion, let me say. Can't handle his booze." Adam scouted the table for a drink but all the cups were empty. Everyone else was coming up from the Ecstasy they had taken while he was away, and so were on nothing but water for now.

Nicola approached, wary of looking Adam in the eye too directly, who was too far gone to be aware he should have been feeling sheepish.

At the back of the room everyone was listening to an anecdote Cat was telling about a model she had recently stayed with in London for the magazine: "…I've never seen anyone throw up so much in my life. She showed me how to do it without putting your fingers down your throat. And where the best place is to shoot smack. It was, like, totally awesome."

Adam was slumped with Cat down on the sofa next to the others, and she had been trying, in vain, to light a cigarette for almost ten minutes, but when she did get the flame of the lighter up, she kept missing the tip of the cigarette. Fiona had even more coke residue under her nostrils now and she stared at the wall opposite, wide-eyed and swaying ever so slightly from side to side.

Adam downed the first of three double Jacks Cat insisted he have.

She had warned him, "I'm either about to dance, or try to kill myself."

Bug asked, "So, Adam. How d'you first meet Fi?"

"She was fucking my cousin Eddie at that Deek fella's party.

128

We met you on the way out."

"I feel like dancing," Fiona yawned.

Bug said, "Knock yourself out, *honey* bun."

Cat's head rested on Adam's shoulder. She had taken too many Es and was starting to pass into freakdom. Her fingernails dug into his arm and she kept saying, "Look after me, will you, Adam? Look after me…"

Adam, oblivious to Cat's nightmare, said to Lucy, "I like Nicholas's outfit."

"Outfit? He's not wearing one. He just got out of hospital. He tried to kill himself…you know, after he faked it. No one realised he hadn't changed before leaving, so he just came as is."

The others were debating the best antidepressants to be on. Cherry said, "You don't want to do Lustral. I heard the funny one out 'Friends' is addicted to that. Watch the new series and tell me you still want to do that shit. Pu-lease…"

Half an hour later – Adam's wish for a pint of vodka finally granted after some begging and cleavage from Cat at the bar – and no sign of Nicola and Trent since they disappeared to the dance floor, Cat was screaming into Adam's ear about books, trying to be heard above the thunderous music, which was so loud, the bass felt like metal rods pistoning in and out of Adam's ears.

"I've decided to write a book," Cat said. "The main character is called Adam. I hope you don't mind…"

He leaned over and put his head in his hands, rubbing his eyes with his palms as he started to cry. "Don't tell me things like that…"

"…it's called 'Cancer Party'…"

The words echoed around in his head. "No, no, it's not," he mumbled, feeling his stomach churning.

"It's quite autobiographical…"

"Please, just stop. I can't cope with autobiographical. Not tonight, please -"

Cat kept on about the motivations of the characters – something about 'ennui' which she insisted on pronouncing as 'Inuit' – and went on to describe some flashback scene.

Adam grasped his temples. "How does it end?"

Cat nodded affirmatively. "The mother dies."

His felt his stomach lurch; it had all gotten too much.

All the toilet cubicle doors were locked except one at the end. Adam pushed it open to find a boy the same age as him sat, pants round his ankles, reading Rimbaud's 'A Season in Hell'.

For some reason Adam didn't immediately shut the door.

"What, do you want a fucking recital or something?" the boy groaned.

"Sorry." He closed the door over and opened the cubicle next to it, only to find the girl he had been with now having sex with Tom, whose devil horns were still strapped to his head, flickering with every thrust. The pair of them stopped and stared at Adam.

He raised his finger in the air, on the cusp of some great proclamation, and sighed, "Would either of you believe me if I told you this isn't the most fucked up thing that's happened to me today?"

The room was spinning, Adam's body pulling him in several directions at once. Nicola and Trent were nowhere to be seen and his grip on the night was slipping away.

He fell over the sofa, spilling his hastily bought drink on Dick who was in mid-sentence: "…talking to this guy about Descartes once. He said 'how can you be sure you're not just a brain sitting in a jar somewhere?'"

Harry sipped at his vodka cocktail. "Good point."

Adam got up very slowly. Dick stared at him, waiting for him to say something, but instead Adam pulled his fist back and punched him as hard as he could in the face, sending him straight to the floor, knocking his jerry curl wig off.

"Adam, have you lost your *mind*?" cried Tom who was just arriving back on the scene.

Harry was kneeling on the ground inspecting Dick's foot. "Look at his spatz. Ohmygod! There's blood on them!"

Adam seemed unaware of any offence. "If we don't exist then I didn't just punch him in the face! He's not even bleeding…well, not much. It's just his fucking cocktail on his shoes. Hey, I'm sorry, Michael." Adam developed a devilish smile and sang, "Look! There's bloodstains on the carpet!"

Cat's eyes were wide with terror, trying to work out if what she was seeing was really happening, muttering to herself, "We might just be brains in a jar…"

Tom and Nicholas waited for Harry to put on his top hat and cane then carried Dick away.

On the floor next to Adam was Tom's pair of comedy devil horns and red cape, which he put on, as he guzzled the last of the drinks on the table.

Adam negotiated the staircase safely and fell out the front door into the freezing cold night air. A heavy frost had fallen since he had gone in several hours earlier; he wrapped the cape around himself, but it amounted to little insulation.

"Adam, is that you?" shouted someone behind him.

He turned around. "Nicola. You should be upstairs dancing. I asked for Michael Jackson but they wouldn't play it."

She smiled. "You're drunk."

He switched on the devil horns and they started flashing. "No, I'm not. Not really, according to Dick."

She took his hand and pecked him on the cheek. "I think I know why you ended up with that girl." Then she ran back inside.

Adam exhaled, then wrapped the cape back around himself and staggered towards the night bus stop.

On the way, a vacant shop window had the words 'Come on die young' etched in dirt on the wooden boarding under an Eton Boys logo. Adam stopped and stared at it, waiting for his double vision to subside. As the words came in to focus he read it back to himself over and over again. He started laughing; He kept laughing until he fell over and was moved along by the police.

Chapter Fourteen

'Carpe Diem and all that'

The devil horns were still flashing on Adam's head when the phone, sitting on the floor next to the living room sofa, awoke him.

He blindly felt around him, picking up a packet of Benson and Hedges, and teased out a dented cigarette, taking a mouthful of flat beer, which he sipped gingerly.

The voice on the other end's elocution was shot through with urgency and agitation. "Hello? Hello, is this Adam speaking?"

A rasping cough followed, along with the reality of his hangover. He felt like he was tumbling down a helter-skelter on a greased baking sheet. "Yeah, who's this? Is this market research again? Are you calling for Mr McNee? This is not Mr McNee, OK? He doesn't fucking live here…"

"Adam, do shut up! This is your Uncle Patrick."

He reached for the ashtray, falling off the sofa in the process, saying, "shit shit shit…". He picked it up again and said breezily, "Uncle Patrick, it's so…*nice* to hear from you. You're up early aren't you?"

Deeply unimpressed, he emphasised, "It's after *lunchtime*, Adam. You never answered my last message so I thought I would call again."

"Yeah, about that. My uh…answering machine was…broken, so I didn't get the message, then the warranty-"

"Do be quiet, Adam."

"OK," he said with acceptance, and started eating some left over pizza on the coffee table, crunching loudly.

133

Patrick recoiled at the other end, taking the phone farther away from his ear. "Adam, where is Edward? He hasn't been home for a week now. You were supposed to take care of him. We're all very upset over here, Adam."

The repeated use of Adam's name was meant to impose some form of respect, something that was never going to come. Adam could always picture the manicured surroundings he was called from, no dust on any visible surface, front lawn mowed in consistent stripes, their carpets hoovered in parallel lines, the chink of fine china chiming from the kitchen…they could never be proper Big Money, and Bearsden had proper Big Money. Adam had found an ease in dealing with his Uncle Patrick, sensing a phoney mask behind those gentle elocutions, that he was really no better than the two-bit local car mechanics he owned, and would never reach beyond the heights of the *auto riche*. Controlling Adam was the best he could manage, and Adam knew it.

"We?" Adam said.

"Yes. Your Aunt Elaine and I."

He paused for another mouthful of pizza followed by more lager. "Well, he ran off, Paddy," Adam groaned, "which is great news as I don't have to share my whisky with anyone now. I don't know, it was all a bit of a blur, to be honest. I remember, we were at this party – Deek something or other – when the next thing I know we were falling asleep on this park bench and these mothers in Burberry were swarming around us like flies." He sniffed, "We were lucky to get out alive, to tell you the truth. They were a bunch of savages. But Crimewatch is on tonight so you never know, he might have just been kidnapped or raped or something…"

A long silence followed at the other end.

"Hello?" he said.

"Are you on drugs?" He half covered the phone to say, "I think he's on drugs," to Elaine in the background. He came back on, "And what the hell are you eating, I can barely hear you?"

"Finishing my dinner from last night, Paddy." He licked his fingers and relit his cigarette. "Look, if he shows up here I'll call you, alright? Now, I've got to go because I'm running low on wine. And you know, carpe diem, and all that, right."

Patrick sounded utterly baffled. "What are you…"

Adam hung up the phone and stared out the window, the curtains still open from when he left the afternoon previous. Everything was still except for the noise of passing traffic on the road outside, the first thing he would notice when he woke up after sleeping in the living room yet again. It was his barometer for the outside world, what time of day it was (he could tell by the frequency of cars passing by), what the weather was like (the rain made it sound like a tsunami was washing its way through the streets, turning it into a shallow canal). That first indicator would shape the rest of his day, whether he would go back to sleep, or go straight to the off licence. Presently there were many car horns, and concentrated periods of shouting from junkie couples, calling out, heads facing the clouds in anguish.

Adam finished his cigarette, stubbing it out on his arm, next to other Braille-like dotted scars that he had made on the night bus home, sticking them in so far and hard as to try to get through to the other side.

The phone rang again and he lunged for the answering machine to switch it on.

The voice blared in, "It's your dad! It's fucking lucky you showed up the other day! We had a good laugh…"

Lucky bastard's drunk already, Adam thought, giving up on the warm lager.

"If you get this just give me a call and I hate to ask, you know, not seen you for a coupla months, and then…you know, but your old man needs some dosh for this fucking gas bill and… fucking… fucking…"

He could hear the pinging of the slot machines from The Crooked Saltire in the background. "And you must be getting that student loan soon! So give us a call back!"

As soon as he hung up the shouting from the junkies continued, a couple screaming at each other over an empty pram, the specifics unclear to anyone but themselves. It appeared that their toddler had simply wandered off when one of them wasn't looking. They kept on and on at each other, Adam watching them at the window, letting his head fall against the glass, his breath forming a cloud of the sparring pair. He stabbed at the delete button on the answering machine message and searched through his personal phone book – an assortment of loose A4 sheets scattered under the coffee table, the numbers scrawled in different colours of ink – trying to find the only person he wanted to speak to at that moment. He had written his name in green ink, just to remind himself: 'DUKE'.

The phone was picked up on the first half of the first ring, as if he was expecting a call. Adam could barely hear down the phone as music was blasting from whichever doss house in Renfrew Duke was now residing in. His voice was strained from a forty-a-day habit; he had smoked everyday since Adam first met him in Primary Five, though Adam could only speculate on what drugs had since ravaged his internal organs since they last spoke.

"Hey, Duke! Yeah it's me. Yeah it's been a while! Too long. What d'you say? How's it going? Aye, fine. What about you? Yeah? (pause) Really? So what are the police saying? Will he get it back? Bummer. So you seeing anyone? Sure, I remember her. 3rd Year Maths class, right. Bit of a goer wasn't she? (long pause) Wow…so when's it due? Uh huh. Right. Nah, thing is, could you sort me out? I know it's been a while…what? For an ounce? Cool. What's that? No thanks. Really, thanks anyway, I don't need any crack. No. No, I don't know anyone who wants crack…I'm on my way over just…Hey, hey don't hang up, you haven't given me the fucking address yet…"

They met outside the house which – right enough – was a doss-crackhouse in Renfrew. The paint was crumbling off the wooden façade and the music was an indistinct rumble from behind the living room, which had tatty, unmatched curtains covering up a set of French windows, one of which was cracked in the shape of an exploding star. Duke's face was white as a ghost and he had lost even more weight since Adam had seen him last. His clothes were bleached and hung lifelessly off him, skeletal, white legs dangling from a baggy pair of beach shorts. His trainers were ripped and his hair had been cropped at the side where he had several stitches protruding. Smoke blew around his face from the huge joint dangling from his mouth, as if he had forgotten about it.

They shook hands, sideways, like ageing hippies.

"Awright, Spaceman?" Duke drawled.

"What happened to you?" Adam asked gesturing at his head.

He took the joint out his mouth and passed it. "Got bottled, didn't I. Cunt just knocked her Bud right over ma bastard head. Fucker." He lightly prodded his head. "Fuck man, *you* look like shit."

Adam took out his money – a small roll of tens. "This enough?"

Duke's eyes lit up. "That's generous, Spaceman." He produced the weed from a side pocket in his shorts and stuffed it in the inside pocket of Adam's tweed jacket. "Any cunt sees you with that stash around here they'll plug you for it. No mistake."

"I'll keep an ear out. Don't suppose you want to buy some downers? I've got this prescription I don't need."

"No thanks, man. Streets round here's flooded with them. Aw these fucking housewives and builders are tossing their loads out in the pubs. I do powders mostly now." He phrased it like he had won a promotion.

Adam speculated, "Scarier buyers, though, isn't it?" and passed the joint back.

Duke shrugged. "Ah fuck it, I'm happy."

They shook hands again and he went back inside. A pregnant girl stood at the front window drinking from a bottle of Grolsch. Adam remembered her face from the school yearbook, but now she was bedraggled and worn-out looking. She still had her hair the same as he remembered, though, the picture that came into his head when Duke described her on the phone earlier. Everyone had wanted her at school - now she was going to be a mum at seventeen. Something about it didn't seem right to Adam; like they were growing up too fast, these children. There was no mystery about their lives, they were all standing at full length windows, their various pains all too clear to see.

She waved to Adam, with a fleck of recognition. (One lunchtime, they had secretly arranged to kiss at the far away school gates, away from everyone else playing on the football pitches. But her friends insisted on tagging along with her, convinced she was up to something. She couldn't afford to let the word get out; to save her embarrassment she just walked straight past him when she got to the gates and lit a fag, shrugging her shoulders at him. He bummed a fag off her and smoked it on the walk back to the football pitches) – he waved back all the same. Duke appeared behind her and wrapped his arms around her swollen stomach. He passed the joint to her and she smiled as she closed the ragged curtains over. Adam could tell they were going to be very happy.

Adam spent the afternoon rolling and drinking heavily, looking out the living room window at the Tanning Salon across the road. *They'll never catch on*, he thought. The same women as usual hung about outside smoking cigarettes, their faces varying shades of orange like the paint samples at Fix It. Slapper Dusklight. Loose Fanny Sunset. Each of them dressed in tight denim miniskirts and low-cut white tops brandishing non sequiturs like, 'Top Class Mum' followed by 'Star' underneath. The tightness of the garments left nothing to the imagination – their fat saucer-like nipples ravaged from breast feeding multiple children, rolls of stomach fat churning around each other. A teenage girl stood next to them, looking bored, pulling on her chewing gum with her finger.

A white Transit van drove past and the men inside hung out the windows and wolf whistled at them as they sped past. "Awright sexy, show us yer tits!" It wasn't clear who the call was directed at.

The driver blew the horn and one of the women called out something indistinct – but definitely encouraging - in the direction of the van. The young girl watched carefully, taking mental notes, then the women went back inside to sit under their cancerous UV lights as a short, heavy rainstorm started.

The kitchen checked out impressively, with a bottle of Totov, eight cans of Tennents, and a Cabernet Sauvignon Uncle Patrick and Aunt Elaine had given Adam as a flat warming present the year before. He had seen it in Safeway the next week for £2.99. Still, it was enough to help him forget for another night.

The pigeons on the adjacent warehouse roof had now made a small nest. They were settling in for winter. Half a bottle of wine disappeared as Adam stood there watching them, until he suddenly remembered what he had come in for: he took the wilting flowers on the windowsill and stumbled downstairs – his head comfortably light and easy – the peephole on Billy's door flashing as he went past.

Some GOMA Kids sat on the steps of the war memorial shouting random obscenities, tossing empty cans at the skater guys, both sets oblivious to the veterans laying wreaths behind them for Armistice Day, unable to concentrate on their prayers for all the yelling and

140

laughing in the background. What fun the GOMA Kids were having!

Adam sat down beside them, waiting for the inevitable call from one of them. A boy wearing a PETA t-shirt beckoned him over, whining for some Flancotex and Kersotap. "They're the painkillers they give to recovering cancer patients, right?" the boys wondered aloud.

"Yeah, that's right," Adam sniffed, and with a flurry of quick hand movements, the money and pills were exchanged. "Make you feel right cosy." And then he staggered away.

Bug and Fiona sat at the edge of the group, kissing too sloppily and hungrily to notice Adam, the joints each of them were holding burning down to their fingertips. Adam looked back at the veterans trying to convince the GOMA Kids to move off elsewhere. A flurry of abuse at the old man followed, his medals and distinction unrecognised.

There were no signs at the end of town, just the sudden sharp rise of the hills – almost like a stunt biker's wall of death surrounding all of Paisley. At the top it levelled out to a plateau to miles and miles of hungry, yellowing fields of grass. The only sound was the wind or the squeaking of grey racers approaching on old bicycles.

Adam's gran had told him the cemetery was built there when the town was still relatively new because the people didn't want death so close to their front doors. Instead, they buried the dead out of the way where the tombstones would be far from view except for lost ramblers or drunk teenage boys. Everyone else would have to remain hidden in UVA sunbeds, behind the twinkling lights of puggy machines in pubs and under the fluorescence of DIY stores. Darkness would never reach them there.

The front gate was a towering iron structure, and behind it, an almost interminably long, straight avenue lined with leafless trees hanging over each side of the road like giant, twisted bones. The wind swirled around the gate entrance, and the now dilapidated band stand where trumpeters and other horn musicians used to play in the old days for the hearses driving in. Rain dripped through gaping holes in its tiled roof onto the rotting wooden floor.

There was no déjà vu upon walking to the back of the grounds, following the trail his mother's hearse had taken. Every thing seemed new, breathing a different air this time, like after a hangover breaks.

Adam was thankful for the drunkenness dawning inside, repeating to himself, "Third row from the bottom, two graves in, third row from the bottom, two graves in…"

Approaching the graveside his pace quickened and he tried not to look at the headstone. It would still read 'Mairi Bernadette – Beloved wife and mother. Died 21st December 1992' like it always had. He dropped the flowers on the ground without breaking stride and didn't look back until he reached the iron gate entrance.

Adam coughed back some weak tears, thinking, 'It doesn't matter, it was a long time ago.'

Chapter Fifteen

'No Surprises'

Next to the burnt out newsagent at the traffic lights, the red in the New Labour election poster was starting to discolour, and Tony Blair's face was fading with every day. Graffiti saying 'The Eton Boys' had been sprayed next to the Icon's face. More had sprung up on walls and bus shelters everywhere overnight – they had actually painted over the GOMA Kids' with a logo of their own: a silhouette of a head with a bowler hat.

With each bus stop Adam passed, there was another logo etched on the plexiglass walls, which no one seemed to pay any attention to.

Nicola and Adam were sitting in a booth in Nice and Sleazy's, which was specked with solitary drinkers, their faces bowed in copies of the NME as Radiohead played on the jukebox; Adam had put in enough money to keep all of 'OK Computer' playing for at least three entire plays, flush from the sale of the Flancotex and Kersotap pills to the GOMA Kids earlier on. 'Paranoid Android' kicked in to its sad acoustic refrain section.

Nicola asked, "Have you had any word from…Edward, is it?"

Adam was too drunk to sit at ease, shuffling about in his sit like a wee boy desperately needing to go and run about somewhere. "My Uncle phoned looking for him and no one knows where he is, basically. I caught him prowling around my uni campus selling fake exam papers. He must be staying with someone. I don't know, I don't get it. He doesn't even know how to cook. He'll probably be found dead of malnutrition under an open microwave in a youth hostel somewhere, a look of confusion etched on his face."

She laughed and fluffed her hair up at the back.

Adam was terrified that Trent would walk in at any second, and assume from her laughter that he was trying to steal her away. He said the only thing he could think of: "Will I get us another tray of drinks?"

"Just what you're having."

In the reflection of the beer fridge, he watched her urgently checking her makeup in a compact mirror. Trent must be coming soon, he thought.

He placed the tray down, all the glasses chiming together, like a chandelier in an earthquake. That's what I am, he thought, a great bumbling earthquake. "There's nothing wrong with my hand by the way," he said.

She narrowed her eyes, unsure at what he was talking about.

"Just in case you thought there was. I don't know what's wrong with it. Nothing really, I suppose." He fidgeted with a copy of the NME someone had left behind on the table.

She asked, "So have you quit uni?"

"Technically, no. It was my lecturer…" He hesitated and cleared his throat, "he uh…well, he killed himself."

"Oh my god. I'm so sorry." She reached across the table but he withdrew his hand, as she had offered him a wasp sting; physical contact had become such a shock.

"How was the funeral?" she asked.

"Cold and wet."

Someone at the bar complained about the 'slash-yer-wrists music'. Adam's head dropped and he closed his eyes.

The bar was filling up with playful hags on the razz, and boozing ruggers, mistaking it for a sports bar. It spurned Adam and Nicola to drink faster and faster themselves; there was clear intent behind their actions. The unspoken resolution to get out of their heads was a way of admonishing what they both wanted to happen later on, when eyelids tended to flap with greater weight, and desire makes itself known as the prospect of an empty bed becomes more and more real.

Adam spluttered something about Trent.

"He's going to a gig in the other place."

"Edinburgh, what's he going there for?" Adam asked incredulous, his elbow slipping off the table he had been so casually resting on.

"I know." She quickly dismissed it. "It's some American hardcore band, 'Roses for Hitler' or something. Apparently the singer's going to kill himself on stage tonight."

Adam nodded. "Cool." Then he remembered about Nicola fixing her make-up, and how she knew they wouldn't be disturbed.

She took out a pen from her bag. "Here. We should each write something on each other."

"What?"

"Come on, it's like word association. You write a phrase or a word on my forehead, so I can't see it, and I'll do the same to you."

"What about the mirrors in the bathrooms?"

"I won't look if you don't."

He paused, waiting for her to flinch, but nothing. Not a flicker. "OK then," he affirmed, reaching for the pen.

145

"Nuh-uh, me first." She took the lid off and pulled Adam's face towards hers.

"You can't make me look stupid, right. Right?"

"I'm writing on your forehead. I could write an equation for perpetual motion on your head and you'd look stupid."

"Is this a water-based pen? Don't lean too hard."

She giggled. "Stop being such a baby."

Some of the other tables were starting to look at them, but luckily drunken bravado was in charge for Adam now. He was just enjoying the feeling of the side of her palm against his cheek. It felt as enormous as a kiss.

She finished and handed him the pen. "There."

Adam had already made up his mind. It was time to go for broke. After all, she wouldn't read it until she got home. He wrote it very quickly, in case she could feel the scribing of each letter: 'I LOVE YOU'.

The other tables looked at them and burst into laughter and scattered applause. Everyone was in on the joke except them. Adam – of course – blushed madly, but Nicola pulled his hand away, forcing him into confrontation; and then he felt his face cool. She wasn't going to let him run away.

A long pause followed along with Adam smirking. "What did you write?"

"I'm not telling you!" she swatted his arm, having to stretch to ensure she made contact. Another pause. "What did you write on me?"

"I'm not telling you either!"

Their heads bowed together, forming a triangle as 'Sugarcube' by Yo La Tengo kicked in from the jukebox. In the silence that followed, the pair of them seemed to agree that there was nothing else left to do but kiss. They had manufactured every other element up that point, and now they had arrived. Their heads fell together like two sticks forming the head of a tepee, and their mouths met.

She pulled back, suddenly aware of what was happening. "I don't know why I had to do that."

Adam reached for the nearest glass, but they were all empty. He cleared his throat and couldn't decide what to look at. "It's alright. There wasn't really anything else to do." He followed Nicola's eyes looking towards the front door, where he noticed Mark from Fix-It standing in profile, then in a flash he was gone, as if moved by an angry director.

"Who is it?" she asked turning quickly to the door.

"It was Mark. Least I thought it was."

"How long has he been standing there?" She had turned paler than usual. "But not long enough to have seen us just now?"

"I don't know."

She took her pen out again. "I smudged yours."

Adam pulled back. "It's alright, it doesn't matter."

"No, I want you to be able to read it when you get home."

A pause followed, only because Adam felt it necessary. "I was thinking, maybe you could read it to me there."

She shrugged. "Yeah, we might as well. There's nothing else to do, is there."

The freezing night air hit them like how Adam imagined a car hitting you, hard at first impact, then soft, working its way through the rest of the body; the alcohol taking its full effect. She took his arm and snuggled into him as they walked down Buchanan Street to the Central Station, dodging the lines of bibbed workers trying to get sponsorship for Cancer Research.

Council workers were putting up the first of the Christmas lights – although it was only mid November – hanging them from one building across the street to another.

"Come on, I want to show you something." Adam took her towards the Gallery where they stood under the white star lights. They were the only ones in the square, and they danced drunkenly around on the steps of the Gallery, locking hands and swinging each other rapidly around and around until they collapsed on the stairs, staring straight up.

Almost as a reflex, Adam took out two cigarettes, passing one to Nicola. "My Uncle Patrick went on safari in Kenya once, and he told me that you can see millions and millions of stars out in the Masai Mara." He gestured at the lights, "It's not quite the same, but still, we've got this. Better than nothing."

They sat down in the living room and Adam turned on the fire. Nicola sat up close to it but she was still shivering.

"I'll get you something till the place warms up a bit." He gave her the jumper he had been sleeping in – a thick knitted one with a design like an old patchwork quilt, the pale flesh of her shoulder showing through a large hole.

She hugged herself as he pulled out a small plastic tea tray where he kept his supplies: many packets of long Rizla papers (better to roll joints with), lighters, bits of card for roach and a little tin with a CND logo on it that he kept his green in.

"I've just got this weed the other day. It's called strawberry."

He handed the joint to Nicola and she lit it, exhaling strongly and blowing a thick cloud into the air which hovered over the coffee table in front of them.

The opening chords of Radiohead's 'No Surprises' flowed out through the speakers as they both slouched down in the sofa, the soft cushions folding in around them. "Seeing as we never got to hear the rest of it earlier on," Adam said, turning up the volume.

Nicola handed him the joint back and rested her head on his chest. "Adam, your heart's racing. Come here." She put her arm around him but this only made his heart race even more. "I'm sorry I panicked tonight, with Mark. This is all just so difficult."

Adam mumbled, "Trent isn't, like, really good friends with Mark, is he? I mean, he probably won't mention it."

She sprung up to her feet, hopping on the spot. "I nearly forgot. I haven't seen what you wrote on me yet." She reached around in her bag and pulled out her compact mirror. "You have to promise not to be too scared when you see what I wrote on you."

Adam couldn't stop staring at the red scrawl on Nicola's forehead, the fear of those three words and the earthquakes they cause, the sudden rifts where once there was respect and happiness. "Maybe this isn't such a good idea," he mumbled.

Nicola lifted the mirror to her face and kept it there for a moment, looking at Adam then back to the mirror. "'I love you.'"

Adam touched his face nervously, from a single prodding finger at his eye turned into his hand enveloping as much of his face as would fit in it. "It was too much, right. Fuck! I'm sorry, I'm so sorry…"

She handed him the mirror.

Adam held it to his face and saw the reciprocal words 'I LOVE YOU' looking back at him, in red italics.

Chapter Sixteen

'An old friend'

The pair woke early and ate cereal together the next morning, watching the morning news with a fat joint, greeted by Tony Blair's enormous, vague smile on the screen.

"I have to go soon. My mother needs turning over," Nicola said. "Hugo's too drunk to do it in the morning."

They walked to the bus stop where everyone was bowed over scratch cards, even old women with waxy hair, almost too weak to provide the back and forwards motion of a coin over the silver windows, to see if, after all these years of trying, they had won the Big Prize and would be able to Escape. To where? And for what? Adam's heart shrunk a little (as if a cold wind was flushing its way through his chest) at such a sight so early in the breaking day. Nicola gripped Adam's hand a little tighter waiting for him to take her to safe ground, beside Littlewoods where they could finish their joint. She kissed him through a cloud of hastily exhaled smoke as her bus appeared. "I don't want to go home, Adam. Really."

"I believe you," he said, the closing bus door almost taking Nicola's hand away. Adam crossed the road to catch his own bus to work, in the opposite direction, out of Paisley.

Fix It drifted by in a haze of cider drank in the staff toilets (smuggled in in an old school flask with a picture of Mickey Mouse on the side with his white-gloved thumb up, a speech bubble above saying, 'Never take sweets from strangers') and two Percocet's worth of ketamine snorted off the cistern. At closing the lights went off in large blocks, the dense rays and constant humming finally relenting

151

for peace. The customers still trying to get in would have to chase their light elsewhere now. Luckily for them there were tanning salons open until ten o'clock.

Adam stopped for groceries at Haddows on the way home, Billy's peephole flashing again as he went up the stairs. This time he cracked the door open.

"Hello, Billy," Adam said, continuing up as the bottles in the carrier bags clanged together loudly.

"Liquid groceries, Adam?"

He laughed but Billy's face stayed straight. "Och, don't be like that now."

"Pretty bonny girl I saw you leaving with this morning."

Adam blushed and looked down, but for once he didn't mind having something to hide. He walked on and Billy closed his door, the phone already in his hand, ready to report back to his usual contact that Adam would indeed be drinking heavily that night, but his spirits would be mercifully high.

At Adam's front door something in the air was different. The air had been disturbed, recently too. He could smell cigars, the door mat had shifted across the landing and there was a great dirty footprint at the bottom of the doorstep. He slid his key in the door but it wouldn't budge. It was already unlocked.

He switched on the hall light, which dazzled him for a few seconds, making him claw at the white spots dancing over his eyes. Dirty footprints trailed from the hall carpet, past a half empty bottle of wine lying on its side, dribbling from the kitchen worktop on to the floor. The bags of booze clanged together again and he winced.

Whoever else was in the flat now knew he was as well. He took the biggest knife he could find in the cutlery drawer and tip-toed towards the living room. The lamp was off but the streetlights crept in through the window, enough to see a man's figure sat in the recliner next to the bookcase in the corner of the room, a brimmed hat on his head which arched to the side. He appeared to be sleeping. Adam raised the knife high above his head – although he had no intent to use it, but his assailant didn't need to know that – and turned on the lamp next to the figure. His face lit up and Adam stepped back, dropping the knife on the floor. There sat Edward passed out in the recliner dressed in a new suit, mirrored aviator sunglasses and a bowler hat.

Adam swiped his hat off and he bolted up in the chair. His reflection shone back at him in the lens of Edward's sunglasses. He stood up with a goofy smile and held his arms out waiting for a hug. "Hello, my little soul warrior. Yoda's back." Without hesitating Adam pulled his fist back and punched him in the face, knocking the sunglasses clean away.

Edward cried out and staggered around holding his nose for a few moments, mumbling *sotto voce*, "owww..." building to a deafening screech, "...ooOW! FUCK!" He dragged his hands down his face. "Yes, that's socialism for you, comrade."

"Times that by ten and you'll get an idea of what happened to me."

"What?"

Adam pushed him back in to the chair. "How did you get in here?"

"I never gave you your spare key back."

153

"I never *gave* you a spare key."

Edward rolled his eyes. "When you were out one day I got one made up, just in case."

Adam paced around the room, unable to contain his anger. "Your dad's going mental. Fucking ballistic, Eddie." He pointed at him. "He thinks I'm to blame!"

"Yes, I know, I know. I *am* aware. That's why I haven't been home, you insufferable thug. He found some…illegal substances. Well! Let's just say when he found out they were yours, he wasn't best pleased." He pulled out a handkerchief with the letters E.B. from his pocket, dabbing at his bloodied nose.

Adam threw himself down on the couch and started building a joint. "Fuck's sake," he said.

Edward held his right forefinger up to signal a pause, and cracked his nose back into place with his left hand. "Footnote: is that a street thing, learning to punch like that so it throbs right through your nose deep into your brain…"

"You're such a bastard, Eddie. Such an invertebrate motherfucker."

He looked at his watch. "Where have you been anyway? I've been here for almost an hour!"

"I was at work. Some of us have to do it from time to time. I want you out, now."

"Adam—"

"You're here for a free bed and you're not getting it. I wouldn't give you a bed of nails. Actually, maybe I would, if you had a tonne weight for a duvet."

"Now look here. You don't understand…" His tone changed to something more alarming. "I'm here to warn you."

"What can you *possibly* have to warn me about?"

He smirked. "You have no idea do you? I knew your smugness would catch up with you. Do you not remember that last morning I saw you? I *told* you about The Eton Boys."

"I remember you selling those exam papers on my campus."

He waved it off. "Tell Trent that it's too late. The Eton Boys are already here. I just had high tea with them this afternoon as it goes."

The toilet flushed next door and Adam spun around to face the door, poised defensively. "Who's that, who's there?"

The figure stepped out from the bathroom, still ringing his hands dry, then went to the kitchen and popped a bottle cork. A boy the same age as Edward stood at the door, dressed in a pinstripe suit and bowler hat. He also wore aviator shades despite the darkness, brandishing a cane in one hand and a glass of wine in the other – a large cigar jutting out his mouth. The light from the hall made him a silhouette matching the logo they had sprayed all over town.

The boy said, "Hello, Adam. I've heard…*so* much about you."

Adam noted where the knife was on the floor. "Great. Another fucking Englishman. What the fuck do you want?"

"My name is Charles. Edward's my friend."

Adam's pupils widened with another glance made at the knife, but Charles quickly spun his cane around upside down and, using the handle, swatted it away with a tut.

"I'm surprised you didn't see me at the university, Adam. Giving those bloody liberals their stupid exam answers. All wrong

155

unfortunately. For *them*. Just wait until their results come back. Daddy will *not* be proud. You see, the time has come to re-establish some natural order around here. At the bottom is you, and at the top is… *will*…be us."

Adam popped a cigarette in his mouth. "I see. No, I understand now. You are both clearly insane."

Charles laughed, "Oh no, Adam. We just want Trent."

Adam stood up to find a lighter.

"Hey! Easy now," Charles warned him, drawing his cane up against his chest.

Adam raised his hands in submission. Charles lit the cigarette with his own silver lighter engraved with the letters E.B. "We've been left no other options."

Eddie said, "We're telling you for your own good, Adam."

"Yes, Edward is most embarrassed about what happened with you and that odious bus driver, so we're doing the honourable thing. We're giving you the warning that no one else will get." Charles took a step forward, moving Adam backwards. "Get out of whatever deal you've made with Trent and the GOMA Kids. It won't last."

"How did—"

"Never mind how I know. *Just walk away.*"

He had Adam backed up flush against the window now, their faces only a few inches apart, the terror in Adam's own wasted eyes reflecting back in Charles's mirrored sunglasses. He has expensive aftershave, Adam thought.

"Don't *tempt* us," Charles sneered, peering out from under the brim of his bowler hat. "There's nothing we like more than a little ruckus. See, it's just so easy to get to people these days."

"What the fuck does that mean?"

Charles planted the brass handle of his cane next to his face against the window with a fresh ping. "There's always a dame… Nicola, isn't it?"

Eddie smirked as he put his hat back on.

"Nicola?" Adam asked. "What the hell does she have to do with this?"

Eddie tapped their two cereal bowls, still lying on the coffee table, with his cane. "Look at this, Charles. Someone had company last night. I hope you used protection, Adam. AIDS is such a terrible disease."

Charles brought his cane back down from Adam's throat. He seemed suitably impressed. "Cute, Adam. Very cute. I expected nothing less. But Adam, girls like her always have secrets…" He lingered in the hall for a second, debating in his mind whether to break something, then shouted back, "We'll await your decision…"

The door slammed behind them and Adam immediately leapt for the phone. He cursed the long connection time, shaking the handset in the deluded idea it would speed up the process. It rang and rang, then finally a beep of an answering machine. It was Nicola's mum's voice.

"Hi, if you're phoning us between ten and lunchtime, then I'm watching 'Good Morning with Richard and Judy', and if you're phoning before five but after one then I'm watching Kilroy repeats or Hugo's watching Channel Four Racing, and if it's after seven…" This continued on and on, with increasingly elaborate television schedules

157

for different times of the day. In the end, they would only come to the phone between two-thirty and two thirty-seven, when the John Stapleton chat show would go to commercial.

Adam slammed the phone down and snapped open a bottle of vodka from the kitchen. Then he looked into the Haddows bag and screamed into his hands "Bastards!". They had taken one of his bottles of wine.

Chapter Seventeen
'Arthur'

They were sat in Arthur's living room having drinks in the afternoon sun – which wasn't registering any warmth whatsoever – by which time Adam had had three shots of whisky and four mini-bottles of cheap beer that were on special offer. It was a waste of time – piss water at a measly 2% proof. Once again he had been followed on my way there. The same person in a brown coat had shown up several times in different parts of town. They stayed far back, normally with the hood up, but Adam had been drunk since midday, and couldn't be entirely sure of anything.

The few days that had passed since Eddie's return had brought about in Adam some sort of 1950s-France obsession with existentialism. "Whenever I look at my hands," he drawled to Cherry, who was busy cutting 'I HATE LIFE' into the inside of her arm, "I can see the world through the other side: I am disappearing; matters running away from me like stray dogs."

"That's nice," Cherry winced blankly, mopping up her blood with a kitchen towel turning ever more red and then black as the blood dried.

Nicola was 'unavailable' whenever Adam called. Her mum told him in between her wheezing breaths, violent coughing, and the delirious cheering coming from the television, that Nicola had gone up to see someone at The Pillbox. *During the day?* Adam asked.

He sat nonchalantly on the floor rolling a joint as Cat discussed her book – something to do with darkness. "See, people will think it's a happy ending, but actually it's not," she explained.

159

Everyone was writing a book.

"*My* book is in its final stages," announced Arthur proudly but everyone was looking out the window as some joy riders went flying past the house, screaming as they tossed their empty bottles out the car window.

"Fucking kids," said Lucy, swallowing a hand full of what may have been relaxants or stimulants. "Right, I've got some homework to do, so…if you don't mind…I'll be over here…"

Dick was oddly quiet – he sat stony faced (still slightly black eyed) in the leather single seater – only lifting his gaze to scowl at Adam.

"My stalker's back," said Cherry searching for a reaction, rolling her sleeve back down.

Everyone has got a stalker.

Only Nicholas responded. "Is Tony still your stalker?"

Lucy cut in, "No, he was mine. Peter's stalking me now."

Cherry pointed her cigarette at Lucy. "Correct. Mine is my ex, Barry. He's in a band."

Cat looked unimpressed. "Oh please, Cherry, everyone's in a band."

"My old stalker killed himself in June," boasted Lucy and mimicked a wrist slashing. "I mean, how pathetic is that? I can't take someone seriously that kills themselves. In any case, no one cuts their wrists anymore. At least have the decency to find a gun or something." She swallowed another Xanax.

Cat agreed, "In London no one kills themselves. They just overdose. At least that way you can still enjoy yourself afterwards."

160

Cherry asked, "Have you got a stalker, Adam?"

He didn't hear her: he had been staring at the bottle of brandy on the mantelpiece for ten minutes, wondering how wasted everyone had to be before he could get away with stealing it.

Cherry turned to Dick. "What about you?"

He paused. "Oh, I'm sorry, Cherry, were you asking me a question or was Adam punching me in the face?"

Adam burst out laughing.

Arthur said, "I wrote a poem about my stalker. It's going to be part of my reading next month.

Cherry asked, "Is that the one at the Drunken Spastic or the Melted Potato?"

"It's called 'Blowjob Queen'..." He then recited the full length of the poem as a joint was passed around in a Royal Doulton porcelain bowl; the imagery was predictable to say the least. Then Tom pointed out the ash might leave an indelible mark on the bowl ('it's very expensive. Very expensive') so Arthur took an ashtray from the mantelpiece above the fire, where a row of internet-purchased prescription bottles sat – the same place he used to stand his debating trophies and prize ribbons.

Arthur finished off: "...So suck, suck, my sweet queen. My sword is solid..."

Then, as the bowl clanged down on the marble, the doorbell rang.

Everyone froze and looked at each other, doing a quick headcount. We were all accounted for.

Arthur put his finger to his lips.

Everyone got down on their knees and quickly shuffled over

to the nearest hiding spot, but Adam remained in plain view in the middle of the room, sitting with his legs crossed, rolling a joint using nine skins, which he didn't plan on passing.

"Adam, hide for fuck's sake!" Arthur said throwing his arms around like a dervish and pulled him over behind the couch.

"Watch the joint, man…"

Cat whispered to Arthur, "I thought your parents weren't coming back until tomorrow, you stupid prick?"

Arthur peeked out from under the window. "I can't see anyone. What if they're hiding?"

The front door rattled.

Arthur tried to hand the joint to Tom. "*I* don't fucking want it," he said and no one else would take it from him. "It's ok, I saw this in a Matthew Broderick movie." So, still lit, Arthur put it in his mouth and immediately started to choke.

Harry shook him like an insolent remote control, smacking him on the back of the head, prompting Arthur to splutter, "My back, you moron, hit me on the fucking back!" He finally coughed it up.

"Just stub it out, you retard!" Harry snapped.

"Fuck you, your parents aren't at the door, man! Your fucking parents aren't at the door, man!"

"We don't even know if it is your parents," Adam said standing up to answer.

"What are you doing?" came the horrified collective response; arms grabbing for his legs.

He picked up the nine-skinner from the floor which has been sitting there like an uneaten cake in front of a starving prisoner. "I want to smoke this thing."

Once in the hall Adam knew who it was through the frosted glass of the door, the slouched posture, the familiar colours of his black t-shirt and AC/DC logo. "It's alright," he said with disappointment. "It's just Donald."

He opened the door.

"Alright, Adam! I've been looking for you. I went up to your flat. And by the way, you left your door unlocked…" He took the joint from Adam's hand and went into the living room. "Alright guys!" he beamed – everyone slumped in their chairs, recovering their breath as Arthur slurped down a glass of ice water. "What's up with them? Oh, I took a beer sitting on your coffee table, I hope you don't mind. Since when do you smoke cigars? And why is your neighbour following me…"

"You mean *Billy*?"

"Cunt followed me all the way here." He passed back the joint.

Adam huffed at the soaking roach he had left him. "Get in here." He dragged him through the hall to the kitchen, speaking in hushed tones. "You can't come here like this, Donald. It's not good for me."

"What's the big deal, man?"

"Circumstances have changed, Donald. This whole thing is out of…look, circumstances have changed."

"Why?"

"Just…*leave*…it, OK?"

Cat, who heard the raised voices, gingerly entered, her eyes rolling about in their sockets. "What's going on?"

Adam gave her a fake smile and an almost caricatured thumbs

up.

She started, "Have you got any—"

"Xanax?" he interrupted, losing his patience. "No, you'll need to ask Lucy like I've told you four times tonight."

She looked at Donald. "And you. You scared the shit out us. What are you doing here?" She didn't wait for an answer and walked back next door.

"What *are* you doing here, Donald?" Adam asked.

"Me and Bug are going to the Virgin Megastore."

He was already opening the door and pushing Donald out. "It's nine o'clock for chrissake. The shops are shut."

"The Virgin Megastore." He paused. "St Catherine's? The all-girl's school. He knows this hot blonde—"

In the living room Cat screamed, "Someone please get me a fucking Xanax! I swear I'll fucking kill myself…"

Adam shut the door in his face and whispered, "I can't handle this right now," and banged his head slowly, but firmly and repeatedly, against the doorframe.

Donald was still talking away, muffled by the door, "…I swear to fuck the sweetest pu–"

Adam started to space out, everything seemed to quiver, vibrating sharply within his field of vision. He wasn't sure how long he stood there against the wall, but the skin on his forehead clung stubbornly when he peeled it back. A smooth, constant swelling burned down to his toes as if his blood had stopped circulating.

In the living room Cat sat hunched over Arthur's computer, her back to Adam, as the others passed a mirror piled with white powder around. They were cutting it with Fix It razor blades – the open packet sitting on the floor.

"Oh, we all thought you'd gone," Cat said. "You nearly missed the coke."

"Oh, well thank god," he said, his sarcasm lost on everyone else. He took the mirror and slipped one of the blades into his pocket when no one was looking.

Dick took the mirror from him and did a line. "Oh, I'm sorry, are you going to hit me again?"

Ignoring the jibe, Adam asked, "What are you doing, Cat?"

She was on the computer scrolling through emails. "Just finishing my column. You know, about my abortion. Figuratively speaking, that is. I'm trying to tone it down. I got all these suicide notes from readers after last month's issue about teenage lesbianism. This one girl said I obviously understood what it means to be totally alone in this world."

Adam responded with a blank, instinctive, "Cool," then realised, "But you're not a lesbian, and you never have been-"

She insisted on reading on: "And you'd better give me another Percocet, the magazine's screening my drugs. They think I'm slacking off. Said my eyes were too lucid for the last photo session; had to spend half an hour with some eye drops and a vinegar shaker." She finished the dregs of a bottle of wine and put it on the floor next to another empty. "I haven't been this thirsty in weeks."

She opened another bottle of wine, and started sharing one of reader's emails: a diagnosis of doom: a minute by minute account of an overdose.

A slow steady drizzle fell against the window, gradually obscuring the view of conifers and Mercedes outside.

"Listen to this," Cat said eagerly, "'...so it won't be long now. The bottles are all empty. Feeling dizzy. No. It won't be long. I hope no one finds me for a long time. Please don't call an ambulance. Just know that you gave me the courage. Thanks.'" She stared blankly at the screen, hand frozen on the mouse. "She died in the end. Her parents sent this on to the magazine, saying 'We know how big a fan of Cat's column our Heather was, and thought you might like this as a small token of our appreciation'. S'nice innit."

Tom, Dick and Harry argued about what music to put on.

Tom was in mid-rant: "...how can you not be in the mood for Romanian heavy metal? You're a fucking philistine, I *knew* it..."

Adam surveyed the devastation around the room; Cherry and Lucy laid next to each other on the floor (they had both become lesbians that afternoon after watching 'Mulholland Drive'), as Arthur fed them coke on the edge of a knife and coaxed them into kissing each other.

Cat fell asleep with a photo portrait of Heather with an incandescent smile on the computer screen. It said: 'Heather 1983-1997' below.

The hi-fi blasted on at almost top volume, a screeching, wailing feedback noise. Tom and Harry sat, nodding their heads enthusiastically, eyes closed. With everyone else passed out, or engrossed in a mirror, Adam simply walked up to the mantelpiece, taking the bottle of Brandy and putting it straight into his bag.

Chapter Eighteen

'I thought drugs made people happy'

Nicola's house was a semi-detached on an estate they called 'Sickie', because there were so many people claiming incapacity benefit off the government – one of whom was Nicola's mum. She had broken her leg five years earlier and stayed off sick an extra six months than was necessary. She called one an 0800 Accident Helpline number and got £8000 compensation from her employer – a small cleaning company – for 'inadequate signage of a step', not to mention a hefty fine from the, now imperious, Health and Safety Executive. Fifty workers got laid off as a result and a year later the company went bankrupt.

During her time off she had discovered daytime TV and chocolate and got fat; trying-to-set-a-world-record fat. Now she was practically immobile and relied on her numerous offspring to take care of her (seven lived with her, but Nicola knew of two others that lived down in England somewhere – forever a pluralist, all of them except the two youngest had different fathers). Nicola was the eldest, so she was given the worst jobs: bathing her, dressing her, undressing her, feeding her, washing her clothes, changing the sweat soaked sheets so she didn't get bed sores...

The streets were filled with hobbit armies of children, covered in dirt, when they should have been at school. A burned-out car lay across the street from Nicola's house. TVs glowed out of every front room window, the coordinated colours of the same show streaming out on to the streets.

Nicola's garden was filled with litter – as was every other house around – and in the driveway behind Nicola's Beetle, sat a clapped out car with the wheels replaced with bricks, so they wouldn't have to pay road tax on it. The house next door had graffiti with the letters 'NF' (for 'National Front') sprayed on the door.

Sweat was bubbling on Nicola's forehead when she beckoned Adam inside.

"Hey, how's it going?" he asked.

She wiped her brow and turned her cheek for Adam to peck. "I'm exhausted actually. Breakfast is just over."

Two small children were running between her legs, firing water guns at each other, soaking the carpet. She scooped them up and dropped them into the living room. Adam swiped some toys and unlaundered clothes off the bottom stair and watched, through the glass door, a middle-aged man sitting on the sofa, dressed in shellsuit made up of five shades of luminous green, filling out a pools coupon, discarded scratch cards lying curled and failed by his feet, which were covered in puffs of silver dust, the removal of which had reminded him that he was a loser, but just one more 'ACE' and he would have been a millionaire. It was therefore crucial for him to keep trying. That was the message. In fact, he relished the scratch cards honesty and encouragement.

A wheezing voice came from above, beckoning Nicola up the stairs, yelling "Turn me, it's time to turn me over."

Adam held Nicola's leg on the stair above as she went past. He peered at the man sitting in the haze of fag smoke. "Who's he?"

"Mum's husband, number four. Hugo."

"Nice guy?"

She shrugged, "Dunno, he's always doped up on Valium. He's clinically depressed. Hasn't worked for two years." Then she suddenly grabbed his hand and took him with her.

At the top of the stairs was Nicola's mum's bedroom, door ajar, awaiting, like a new circle of hell Dante daren't describe. The curtains were drawn, but a shaft of bright afternoon sunshine broke through a gap in the middle, lighting a huge blob of a woman, something that had only ever been seen in Roger Corman's nightmares, indistinguishable from the dozens of pillows and cake wrappers that propped her up. The bed frame appeared to be reinforced with the sort of metal bars installed in a rally car's roll cage.

The Fat Nightmare talked out the side of her mouth, in a thick, suet pudding dialect. "Geez some more of them caramel chew things, widya?"

"Hi, I'm Adam," he said, inexplicably holding out his hand.

She grabbed it (true with sweat) and pulled herself up with a long groan. "Prop me up widya, son?"

Nicola asked cautiously, almost hiding behind the door, "Are you going to see your physio today?"

"Mebbe," came the response.

"Right, come here and help me roll her over," Nicola said to Adam.

He tried to keep his hands on the duvet, but as soon as the Fat Nightmare started moving, her whole momentum stretched the linen to breaking point, before snapping back, revealing a continent of spottily blemished, cracked flesh, her nightie riding an unfortunate distance up her legs. It was like watching a whale trying to escape the

169

sea.

Adam crouched down to avoid looking at 'it', putting his shoulder into it, until finally she popped out the pothole she had created in the mattress overnight, quickly diving forward like a Landrover breaking out of a deep ditch. Adam wiped his hands down on his trousers. He felt like he had put weight on just getting involved with touching her body, even observing her he felt full up.

The Fat Nightmare now rolled over (the sodden sheets peeled back, desperate for the washing machine) she clattered her feet down on the ground, her nightie dripping off her like a tent. It must have been at least three days since she had last bathed (she smelled like chicken), and her hair hung tangled like a well worn mop. She waddled over to the window and opened the curtains (Adam was still trying to forget her fat arse). Out of breath, she said, "Is my wheelchair ready downstairs?"

Adam always wondered if people like her were fat because they were in wheelchairs, or in wheelchairs because they were fat.

"You're not going to get back to work without your physio," Nicola sighed.

"I'm no feelin well enuff th'day."

"You know, not everyone gets to see a physio."

She gestured at the TV where a man was leaping across a miniature of the United Kingdom floating on a river outside a television studio. "Put it oan three, son. Richard and Judy's doesnae finish till lunchtime."

Adam sniggered, thinking of the answering machine message. "Em...it's after one."

170

"A'ready?" she huffed. "Where's the day goan?"

"You didn't eat it did you?" he mumbled.

Nicola slapped me lightly on the arm, imprisoning a smile. "I'm going out for a bit with Adam, mum."

"Who the hell's Adam?"

He mumbled, "Me."

Clearly unimpressed, she waddled off to the bathroom with the assistance of a silver walking stick. It was unclear if it was to help walk or to dislodge secreted sweet papers from unspoken orifices (hers had the tendency to drift and swell like the sea).

The Fat Nightmare shouted, "Dinnae be long. And mind Hugo's prescription…" then slammed the door shut. After a few seconds there was another thud.

Adam looked concerned. "Is she alright?"

Nicola dismissed it. "That's just her sitting down on the toilet."

"I think I know why you've always got Valium in your car now."

They went downstairs where Adam waited with Hugo in the living room as Nicola changed. Hugo sat in a single seat chair watching horse racing, but with the sound off. He dragged his one solitary long fingernail (his scratch card finger) over the same ridge on the arm rest to clean the silver dust out - the only discernible noise.

Adam sat on the extreme edge of the farthest away seat. The cigarette smoke in the room was so thick it was difficult to breath; the television screen looked like it was coming via Mars the picture was so woolly; the woodchip on the wall was coated with a tarry residue. They sat and watched an entire race in silence, from the paddock to the interview with the winning jockey: all smiles and muted elation.

171

Hugo leaned forward and squinted, analysing the screen carefully, then he tore up his coupon. I pleaded for the noise of Nicola coming down the stairs, but every time it was just another child.

"Are you scared of silence, son?" Hugo asked suddenly.

"Eh...no, it's quite nice."

"Most folk are scared a silence. They don't know what to do with themselves. So they try ae fill the space by talkin rubbish." He eyeballed Adam. "You're not going to sit there and talk rubbish ir ye?"

"No. Not if you don't want me to. It's your house, man."

He looked up at the ceiling (the bedroom above) as it creaked and picked up another coupon off the arm rest as a new race was readied. "She's always oan at me, 'turn oan they lights. Ye cannae say a thing in here.' I say, leave em! Don't even need 'em." He kept staring at the TV. "I'm Hugo."

"Em, Adam."

"Hello, Em, Adam," he laughed to himself, amused at his joke. He abandoned the ridge on the armrest to twirl a small bookies pen between his fingers, back and forth with dazzling virtuosity. He had obviously spent hours perfecting.

"Ye one of them fucking hippies she hangs out wiff?"

"Yes."

He looked at Adam for the first time. "Ye should get her away fae here."

"Nicola?"

"Who else?" He shook his head. "D'you like my house?"

"Yeah, definitely."

"You can have it then." He laughed and lit a cigarette. "I know

172

what you're thinking. It was when you saw her," he looked up at the ceiling, "right? You thought, 'that guy must be really ill to stay here.'"

"No! I didn't…"

His hands were visibly shaking as he rubbed his pallid face. "It's awright. Things are gonna to get better…" He seemed to drift off for a second, and muttered quietly, like he was having a conversation with someone next to him.

"Em…Hugo?" Adam mumbled.

He shot up in his chair and his eyes widened. "Nicola," he announced.

"Yeah?"

"D'you love her?"

"Course."

He sat back, as if exhausted by the slight movement. "If ye love her, then ye'll get her awae fae here," he said then he shut his eyes and immediately fell asleep.

Nicola stood in the living room doorway. Adam wasn't sure how long she had been there behind him. "Ready?" she asked.

"Yeah, just a sec," he said, waiting for the race to finish. He went across to check Hugo's coupon against the winner, then tore it up for him.

They held hands all the way back to Adam's.

He asked, "What happened to your dad?"

"In a country rock band in Canada. My mum was a groupie." She walked with her head down for a while, and dodged the cracks in the pavement. "I've always wondered if it's wrong to hate your own

173

mother?" she asked.

"God. I don't know." He paused. "She doesn't seem like much of a mum to me, Nicola."

She swallowed hard, hard enough for it to appear to echo around all the seemingly infinite concrete that surrounded them. "Do you hate your mother? You know…for dying?"

He paused. "It was a long time ago."

"I know that, but do you…" she trailed off. "Seemed like you and Hugo had an interesting conversation. So he reckons we should get out of here."

"You heard?"

She stopped walking and tightened her grip on his hand. "You *love* me?"

"Course."

"I don't know why."

Chapter Nineteen

'White Light'

When he woke the next morning, he reached across the bed expecting to feel Nicola's white body next to his. The bed sheet retained her shape in it. Having slept the longest he had in months, he was exhausted, not knowing what to do with his limbs to relieve the pain in his joints. It was only after he tumbled out of bed and opened the curtains – taking a moment to survey the utter stillness outside – he realised that love had finally flowed through his body.

Against the weather forecast, heavy snow had fallen overnight. From the white clothes lines hung cleaner's and supermarket uniforms; the lines were camouflaged by the snow on the ground, so the clothes appeared to float in mid-air – disembodied and lifeless bodies hanging from gallows, exhausted with love, with love. The pigeons pecking around on the warehouse roof were the first things he noticed move, being set upon by an albatross. He banged the window so hard as to cause snow to fall from the window sill outside. "Get away from them!" he yelled, with the veracity that one only reserves for the defence of family members.

A note sat on the kitchen counter, written on the back of a Haddows receipt. It said, 'I'm sorry I've run off. Mum will be needing to get up soon anyway. Things are really confusing now. I didn't expect to hear you say that you love me. I don't deserve it. I just need a few days to myself.' She signed it with an 'N' then an 'x'.

All that was left of her now was the jumper she had worn the night before, lying in a ball by the foot of the bed. Adam picked it up and held it to his face – the smell of her perfume was still on the collar

– long enough until he ran out of oxygen and had to release it. The scent rose up inside him and it felt like the sting of his first shot of whisky that morning.

Sitting in front of Adam on the bus was a loud, brash mother with her son, no more than four or five. The boy was crying, but she just threw him recklessly over her shoulder and carried on talking to her gormless girl friend. They talked of nothing; only in prepositions, like they had no idea what to feel about anything, the vastness, the bigness of everything: they weren't built for it: "And I was like *that*, and he went, like, pure…"

"Waiter, can I get a noun over here please!" Adam said, prompting some concerned stares from the man across the aisle.

Adam smiled, then held the jumper Nicola had been wearing up to his face and breathed in hard. The scent was already beginning to fade.

The little boy started giggling at Adam as he hid his face behind the jumper, then he pulled it away and said, "Peekaboo!"

The boy laughed and pointed at Adam hopefully. "Daddy?"

Adam shook his head. "Sorry. I don't even think mummy knows who daddy is."

She turned around slowly, and with a growl. Adam put the jumper back up to his face and sat back.

Adam had expected Argyle Street to be packed with early morning, wallet-clutching shoppers, eager to spend their hard-earned money now that interest rates were finally falling, the recession receding on the back of the wave of Cool Britannia optimism. Instead: The wind whistling litter around at head height (bat it away); dawn slowly filling the empty glass corridors of streets with thick juicy light (shield your eyes). Lonely people in white jackets stood in front of every shop door, shaking buckets of coins, saying to no one: "Cancer Research, Cancer Research," (just tell them you are the afflicted; they'll understand, Adam).

He was sweating heavily with paranoia by the time he reached Debenhams. Several blonde girls that looked like models floated around in front of the escalators, offering him instant store credit.

"Excuse me sir, would you be interested in 0% finance today-"

"I'm sorry I don't have…I'm not…just please leave me alone," he stammered.

He raced past people by climbing the already fast-moving escalator to the perfume department. His desperation was exacerbated by the empty aisles, everyone's sales efforts concentrated on his withered soul: his hair dishevelled; faded, torn jeans; emitting a general smell of marijuana and trouble. *What's that rag he's carrying around?* None of the signs giving directions seemed to make any sense.

His heartbeat steadied amidst the silvery clouds of Calvin Klein, Tommy Hilfiger and Hugo Boss being squirted into the air. The pretty counter girls offered assistance but he jumped back at every one, his face burning red, then lurching in to another beauty queen with her lies of 'hello, *sir*'.

Adam started ranting, mostly towards the floor, "How about I pay you your commission right now, and then we can start to be honest with each other. It will relieve you of any sense of obligation you might have to respect me and my ugly, ugly face; my skinny, skinny legs. I can tell that you are one those women that is used to being held long in to the night, cradled by big strong arms, sinewy triceps, muscular tongues that practice Olympic oral sex." Adam moved on too quickly for the woman to respond in any way, except to dial her phone for security in a rather panicked fashion.

As soon as he got near a counter he coughed and spluttered between words, all the while waving the jumper around like an epileptic as if to stress the point. "This jumper...I...ACGGGHH!... I...BLURRRGH! need this (cough)...on..."

The women looked at their colleagues for help. "Em...I don't-"

"OK, never mind..."

Next booth down: a pretty brunette squirted a bottle of something in the air, and when Adam felt the tiny drops hit his face it was like that first shot of whisky again. It was heart-shaped, and had a black arrow through it. The words at the bottom said 'White Light'. She crooked her head to the side and stared thoughtfully into Adam's eyes.

"What...em...can I take one bottle of...em...this, please?" he said, wiping the light glaze of sweat from his forehead.

"This one? White Light?" she asked. "We have some...better quality perfumes here if you..."

"I want this one," he stressed, crossing his arms tightly, holding down his hands underneath to stop them shaking as security waited in the wings, ready for any trouble. "No, no this makes sense," Adam spluttered, "because Nicola couldn't afford anything else."

Collapsed. Shivering. Foetal position now. In bed. Jumper curled up beside him. Joint like a cone. Burning in an ashtray. The heating was off. Off all day. Whisky was cheaper (it got him thinking, was it possible to drink the fluid in his radiators? Would that get him high? Could he phone a plumber to check?). Breath visible in the mirrored wardrobe. Switch on the light box on the floor. Eyes instantly recoiled for safety. Eyelids failure to respond to brain's demands for them to close. Eyelids had gone on strike. This fucking country.

He placed the bottle of perfume next to the ashtray – and for the first few minutes his light box hummed away quietly beside him; a warm light filled up every cell of his body. The room glowed the clinical white of a psych ward. He sprayed some of the perfume on the pillow and pulled down his boxers. His legs were red raw with cold.

Only half hard he forced out a stilted orgasm, the joy of which left as quickly as it came; weak and fleeting. It probably realised it was far too cold to come out and just lay on his stomach for five minutes while he regained his breath.

A flurry of car horns woke him late the next day. He had entombed himself in a duvet on the recliner in front of the living room window, with vague recollections of the night before: the dried scabs of cigarette burns on his arm suggested a passage of at least twenty four hours, as did the empty bottle of vodka on the floor, and the dried blood (*my own? some animal's?*) under his fingernails. A draft leaked in through the windows; the sun surging bright then dim as clouds sprinted across the sky.

The phone started ringing and the answering machine took it.

The person started with a sigh: "God, machine again. Adam, this is your Uncle Patrick. *Again*. Just to let you know Edward has been in contact with us and told us *everything* that went on when he was there with you. Needless to say I will be calling your father about this matter, if someone can drag him away from the pub long enough to answer his phone. Or has he been cut off again? *Anyway*, Edward told me all about you selling his watch, and yes, I know about the drugs. Goodbye, *Adam*."

"Wait!" he shouted as he ran for the phone – somehow trying to unwrap himself – but he hung up before he could pick up. He yelled, "I'm going to kill you, Eddie!" then tripped on the duvet, knocking over tenpins of beer bottles on the floor.

What I really need is some Lustral, he thought. *My stomach wouldn't burn if I had Lustral. And maybe some Seroxat.* He opened his weed tin and built a paper breakfast. And there was still some vodka in the fridge, so he took a shot of vodka and put some miniatures in his shoulder bag along with the White Light perfume. It was the very least he needed to make it to work.

Chapter Twenty
'O Flower of Scotland'

The Barras market brimmed with the cattle of shoppers and football fans on their way to Parkhead to watch Celtic. "They do love their mindless distractions," Adam said to himself. They drank openly in the street but there were too few police to arrest everyone, so they all got away with it.

Due to his fear of nameless narrators in books, he sat down on a bench – next to a row of winos – to have the first of his miniatures, and immediately felt compelled to introduced himself to his toxic peers. "I'm Adam," he said simply, to a few nods from those who were still hearing human voices. Now he could settle down and have a good drink. He admired their strength of will not to indulge in weightless frivolities like the weather. *Who gives a shit? Look at the sky: it's gonna rain isn't it!*

A Glasgow City Sightseeing bus drove past them. A throng of tourists leaned over the edge of the open-top roof, snapping photos with their long-lens Nikon cameras. They pointed at the drunks, one of them clamping on an extra-long zoom lens, trying to get the labels of their booze in frame.

He directed them: "You...smile? Ja? Ja? Hold up can? Ja, that's it!"

The old drunks held up their bottles of tonic wine triumphantly and the whole bus cheered. Some Neds in green tracksuits, drinking bottles of Buckfast ran across to the bus, and the tour guide nervously tried to usher everyone to the other side of the bus – he had seen this before – but they were all too busy singing 'O Flower of Scotland' in pidgin English as the winoes conducted them. Then the tourists made the mistake of putting on their oversize Union Jack 'jester' hats and started shouting, "Rule Britannia! Ja! Ja!"

The Neds, mistaking this as some Unionist slur, threw coins at them. "Fuck you, ya Orange bastards! Bobby Sands youse cunts!"

One tourist was hit in the face and fell down, dropping his camera over the side, smashing on the pavement as blood trickled from his face.

"Aw yass man!" the Ned shouted as they shook the bus as hard as they could, trying to topple it over as it sat prostrate at the traffic lights. "No surrender!"

The bus driver hit the accelerator anyway, despite the red light, and the tourists were thrown backwards. Other tourists on the street quickly started walking back towards the city centre with their tartan shopping bags. No one had told them about this shit, this shit.

All Adam heard for the first half an hour at work from customers was, "Right, ta."

"Right, ta."

"Right, ta."

It continued like the throbbing buzz of the fluorescent lights. Nothing to say for themselves. Any thanks was completely trancelike, not out of empathy, but regimental duty. No eye contact. Disapproval of hands touching when moneys exchanged.

A little girl of about five ran in with her mum and dad and raced towards the back of the store. Her face beamed, whispering in awe. "Look at all the pretty lights mummy! Look at all the pretty lights!"

Her mother whisked the girl away as if she had misbehaved or uttered slander.

He was sitting alone in the canteen reading, when Spencer Brown, the Regional Manager, entered.

Already drunk, Adam mumbled, "Great, just what I need…"

Spencer smiled cheesily, then as if he was presenting himself to a roomful of people, shouted, "Hi!"

Adam looked over his shoulder, then around the empty room.

He was wearing comedy Rudolph antlers which he pointed to and giggled to himself, "Antlers…"

Adam rolled his eyes.

Cheryl sat next door in the smoker's room with Paul who smoked a roll-up cigarette. She was trying to get his attention by tickling him with some red tinsel she had draped around her neck, but he kept batting it away.

Spencer wandered over. "What's your name?"

"Adam."

"Hello, Adam, nice to meet you." He held out his hand but Adam continued reading. "So, where's your apron?"

"And right there, we get to the heart of it."

Spencer looked towards Cameron Marshall – one of several assistant managers – for assistance with this young fellow who wasn't playing along. Cameron hesitated, "Spencer, we've got lots to show you, let's see the-"

"Not yet, Cameron. I'm just talking with little Adam here."

Cameron gestured for Adam to keep quiet then said genteelly,

"I don't think Adam has anything to say, actually."

Spencer reassured him. "I'll just be a second." He kneeled down beside Adam and lowered his voice, "It's just…you know you're meant to keep your apron on up here, just in case…you know, a customer…were to…"

Adam slammed his book down causing Spencer to visibly jolt. "Were to guess the password on the door entry, making sure none of the hundred-odd cameras in the store didn't see him or her doing so, find their way up the stairs, assuming that not *one* member of staff is going to stop and ask, 'Hey, what the fuck are you doing here?', then go into the canteen, where even the microwave is nailed down, only to be appalled that I don't have my apron on – because this particular customer with a penchant for cat burglary and trespassing finds that kind of behaviour *really* offensive? Just in case *that* were to happen, that's your position?"

He nodded and cleared his throat. "I take on board what you're saying, Adam. And I'm *listening*. Perhaps Cameron can clear this up later."

Adam knew already what it meant. Spencer wanted him fired for the insult.

Cameron chimed in as if to absolve himself of any guilt in their coming sit down. "Health and Safety isn't it, Spencer, Health and Safety."

The words had lost all meaning to Adam.

Spencer gathered himself. "So, what are you reading?"

"*The Twits*," Adam sneered through gritted teeth.

Spencer laughed nervously. "Ha, ha. That's a good one. Anyway,

I should be getting to River Oak Warehouse and see how the repairs are going." Then he walked into the smoking room and made the same introduction: "Hi, guys…" he laughed and pointed, "…antlers…"

Cameron pulled Adam's book down from his eyes. "You've got a serious attitude problem, Alan."

"Do you mind? I'm trying to read."

He stormed off after Spencer and didn't bother holding the door for Cheryl as she passed him. Her ponytail was tied back with her red tinsel and she wore a badge that said '19' on it.

"You OK?" she asked.

"Yes, I'm…fine."

"It's just…your hands are trembling."

Adam looked at the edge of the pages, they were waving all over the place. "It's just…" he trailed off unable to think of an excuse.

She took the book from him. "Hunger by <u>Nut</u> Hamsun."

"Knut. It sounds like 'newt'."

"Bit of a stupid name isn't it?"

"Yeah. Well, he ended up a bit of a Nazi, so maybe there is justice in the world after all."

She slid her chair closer to me. "It's my birthday today."

"I see from your badge, congratulations…I mean, well done… or just, happy birthday."

She stared blankly at him.

"I'm sorry I didn't get you anything, though. You can eh… have my book if you like. Or I'll buy you a book?"

She looked worried at the possibility. "Em, maybe…just buy me a drink, that would be fine."

Mark entered, mumbling something about a hangover. "I feel like a fucking traffic accident."

Cheryl read the blurb of the book. "This sounds pretty depressing," she said handing it back.

Adam protested mildly, "I…I guess I always thought it was more-"

But she was already at the door, flirting with the Flannel Shirt that drove the Corsa, fingering the tinsel in her hair as he kissed her.

Suddenly Adam wanted all those stories about UFOs existing to be true. *Maybe*, he thought, *everything would be better that way, if maybe they took me away. I'd let them do experiments on me. I don't care.*

Cheryl said something about him giving her her birthday present once they got home. Then they giggled with each other. Adam couldn't concentrate on the words in his book anymore. He had reread the same sentence ten times now: 'Despite my alienation from myself at that moment, and even though I was nothing but a battleground for invisible forces, I was aware of every detail of what was going on around me'. Each time he was halted by images of Cheryl furnishing the Flannel Shirt with fellatio, gurgling about what happened in Eastender's earlier with his cock still in her mouth.

His face burned red, which worried him, in case someone thought he was reading a dirty book. *Why else would I blush? Does 'Hunger' sound porny?*

Mark sat across from him, and poured a miniature whisky into his coffee. They managed about ten minutes, alone, in silence, pretending they hadn't really seen each other at Sleazy's the other

186

night; that he hadn't seen his boss's girlfriend cheating with a skinny alcoholic like Adam.

He finally spoke, pausing between mouthfuls of microwaveable curry. "She'll never fuck you."

"What?"

"Cheryl. She's been fucking Paul for at least a month now."

The Flannel Shirt has a name! Adam thought. "Really."

"I can get you a tape if you like. Of them banging. Rob in security caught them on camera in the timber yard. Says he's going to sell it on the internet and become a millionaire like Branson."

"Well that's what they want, isn't it. It's so we all become millionaires and the entire country will have to pay 50% tax."

"I suppose so."

Adam paused. "So…Trent then?"

"Yeah."

"You help the GOMA Kids?" Adam decided if Mark was going to ignore the scene with him and Nicola, then that was fine.

Mark wiped the corner of his mouth with a paper napkin. "I help who I can. I hear things." He looked up at Adam and glowered. "I see things, too."

Adam's heart lurched. "Oh yeah. And what do you see?"

A long pause. "The Eton Boys," he said nonchalantly, with a smile.

When Adam got back downstairs, Sheila handed him a length of thick elastic cord with a hook on either end and sent him to the car park, which everyone called 'Coventry'.

Adam looked at the rope blankly. "What? Do you want me to

hang myself?"

Outside, a chubby little kid with steamed-up glasses, battled with a pile of twenty or so trolleys against the wind and rain. Every time he tried to push the trolleys forward, a few fell off the end, and he had to run down and catch them before they collided with any cars. Then the ones at the *other* end would fall away and he had to catch *them*.

Adam ran over. "You can go inside now. Angus, right?"

He had a thick lisp. "Oh thankth. It'th really hard out today," he said. "The airth really denthe and I can't breath right…"

He wheezed as he walked away inside.

A few of the building team hung around outside the Trade door at the other end of the car park. They shouted at him, "Run Forrest, run!"

He feebly tried to shout back at them but he couldn't muster the breath. He broke down on the edge of the pavement, the car park practically empty.

Adam sat next to him. "Hey, don't listen to them, Angus. They're wankers. If you cry, they think they've won."

He smiled and gave Adam his fleece. "Thankth, Adam." He had huge, clumsy eyes, the kind they put on toy animals to instantly make you want to hug them.

For the next two hours Adam toiled around the car park in the pissing rain, dodging cars that would drive straight at him. A customer drove away, having abandoned their trolley (filled with litter) in the middle of a space so no one could get in.

Adam shouted after them, "No wonder Communism never

took off in this country! Hugh MacDiarmid warned me about people like you! Maybe he was right about something."

It was only after about half an hour of toil, that Adam realised the cord was for keeping the line of trolleys together. He delighted in explaining to people: "You know, I'm not only a trolley boy, no, no. I normally work on the tills…" and "I hope you don't mind me asking but, is that White Light you're wearing?"

After his shift he snorted some more ketamine in the toilets. Visibility outside had deteriorated to only a few yards in front of him as a thick fog enveloped the car park. Walking through the Barras, a deep paranoia consumed him as the pubs approached chucking-out time - voices approached and passed him without a body being seen. When he did catch a face, each was more terrifying than the last.

A hooker staggered towards him, her face badly bruised. "Lookin for business, luv?"

He paused and considered the offer. "You want me to pay you to give me crabs?" he asked. "Tempting, but no thanks."

No matter. She stopped the next man leaving the pub. They talked for a few seconds, then when he looked back they were fading into the mist, walking up the alley behind the pub. She had probably called him 'stud' or 'cowboy'.

At his bus stop Adam convinced himself an old man with a stick was the Grim Reaper. Every time Adam tried to see his face the man turned away, as if trying to protect his identity. Adam tapped him on the shoulder and the old man whipped around, snarling, "Widdya wan…!"

"Sorry, I thought you were someone else," he said.

Chapter Twenty-one

'Dog'

The Abbey was a coal black building, one of the tallest in Paisley, and sank into the night. Adam sat on one of the marble benches that lined the edge of the Abbey gardens, enjoying a brief moment of calm, of headlights seeking out the fog, swooping through like submarines. The town was hushed quiet, except for the stop/start scrape of the skateboards of GOMA Kids on the marble paving slabs in front of the Abbey. Adam didn't recognise them. Everyday there seemed to be more of them.

A stray dog ran around the skaters, barking madly in a husky rasp, its ribs poking through translucent skin. The Kids stopped their tricks and beckoned it over. As one of them petted it he grabbed hold of its neck but it wriggled free and scurried for freedom. The boy threw his skateboard at it, catching it in the back of its head. The dog's bark turned to a low-pitched howl and it fell instantly. The gang skated across and huddled over it, taking turns to kick it in the face and body, yet its cries did nothing to rouse me; Adam looked on merely to see confirmation of the result (inevitable): defeat, lying broken on the ground, more defeat. He shook his head as the New Labour poster from the bus route flashed into his memory, that of an invincible smile, one that shone the truth like a light.

They placed the dog's scrawny, unfed leg up onto the edge of the kerb, then jumped on it, snapping it like a pencil. He then took off its leash and throttled it. They all laughed as it choked, then he finally let go as it drew near its last breath. If only the dog was bigger, then they could all have some fun and not have to wait patiently for their

191

turn. They each raised their skateboards up high, then brought it hurtling down on the dog's head. After two or three blows it stopped whimpering. A boy pulled a knife and plunged it almost mercifully in to the dog's stomach, dragging it up to its chin - just to make sure. Then the boys left. A gentle but constant stream of blood flowed from the dog's belly and trickled away down the drain.

There were no stars or moon visible that night; the sky was a mix of matt orange and grey. Adam stood over the furry heap on the ground, looking back and forth at the streets surrounding him, a solitary figure in a familiar brown jacket standing at the foot of the High Street in profile, hurrying off before further identification could be made.

Adam sniffed with sadness and nudged the lifeless dog on the ground with his foot. One of its ears was ripped in half, and the other, almost completely severed, hung on by the thinnest thread of cartilage. Its coat was soaked with blood, its legs broken and shattered. He took it off the marble and laid it down on the grass as a street sweeping cart approached. The driver – blank, dark glasses despite the darkness - swooped down the brushes and vacuum, sucking up the flesh and chipped tooth then drove off, leaving a blood trail behind it. And so Adam left, the result now confirmed. Defeat, defeat. And he had done nothing. This he knew.

Adam's footsteps echoed around the stairs as he jabbed them slowly and sharply into each one and rapped on Billy's door. The peephole lifted and his shadow peeked under the door frame, but he took several seconds to open.

"Adam. It's a little late," he said rubbing his eyes pretending he'd just woken up, his cheeks still rosy from cold. A brown coat hung from the wall behind him.

"Sorry."

"Is that blood on you?"

"It's OK, there was this dog…I just wanted to tell you…" Adam breathed in hard, "you don't need to keep following me. I mean, I know that-"

"Uh…what?"

"It was my sister, wasn't it? Did she ask you to do it?"

He paused for a second. "I'm sorry, Adam. She's just…been calling all the time…and I am a friend of the *whole* family-"

"It's alright, Billy. And next time you speak to my dad…och forget it."

He nodded.

Adam's voice was empty, even quieter, even softer than usual. He sounded like bones rattling in an empty cage. A rapidly emptying bottle of whisky hung by his waist, held with two crooked, despairing fingers. "Well, alright. Goodnight, Billy," he droned, turning away before he could see the tears forming in his eyes.

"Adam, I'm sorry," he shouted up to me.

"It's fine," Adam replied, not looking back. As soon as he got in he set about spraying White Light around each room of his flat, and like any other drug addict he found himself needing more and more to get this same effect. He guzzled booze as if in a desperate bid to drown his tonsils. Tears were flowing from his eyes – not the cute, perfect sort that trickle out down a movie actor's cheek at the moment of emotional impact and when the score is rising; these were waterfall-tears, flash flood-tears. He started beating his face, unable to smell the perfume for his dripping nose. His tears were 50% proof, now mostly booze when he tore the cap off the bottle and sniffed in lungfuls straight from the source. He sighed in abject pain, his chest heaving and expanding, heaving and expanding faster than he could catch up with, all the blood in his body fallen towards this toes; it appeared he had no need for it anymore. After some minutes this became too tiring a process, and so instead started guzzling the perfume, drinking it straight from the glass tip, setting off a blistering panic in his brain, and agony in his stomach.

He collapsed back into the sofa, looking up towards his ceiling, when he smiled, gently breaking into a snigger, then a laugh, as snow began to fall on his head from some unseen black cloud. He held his arms out to catch the soft flakes, his eyes wide with wonder, taking several seconds for each word: "I…hope…this…winter…never…ends."

Chapter Twenty-two
'The Flyover'

It was almost eight and the sun had set several whiskies before. How quickly the darkness came. From his bedroom window Adam could see the motorway in front of the old industrial estate where his dad and Frank had worked - before the drinking incident. Cars raced over the flyover; only the red and white lights visible, as the road fused with the blackness of night – as if they were somehow cut off from the road, and were gliding through the night of their own volition. Adam noticed his glass was empty again (refilling it was becoming a full-time occupation) and poured out some more vodka, adding a dash of White Light, just to brighten his skies a little. He saw himself on that flyover, surrounded by the red and white lights whizzing past his hips, the sound of aeroplanes escaping from Glasgow Airport throbbing in his eardrums. "Why the rush, man?" he yelled through the window, the heat from his breath forming a brief mist on the glass. All those lights, all those lights.

Adam arrived at the Old Mill to find Bug crouched down in the crunchy frosted grass in front of the chain link fence surrounding the now dilapidated building – Fiona and Donald sat a body's length away from him on a sheet of flattened cardboard (Adam could make out the familiar orange face of the Monster Munch crisp monster that had shaped so many primary school playpieces when he was a boy), necking a bottle of Frosty Jack cider. Two already empty bottles – the plastic bodies of which had been strangled by Donald's fist – lay next to them. Fiona was struggling to roll a joint in the freezing cold, her fingers too stiff to roll the papers satisfactorily.

Bug was hopping and prowling up and down the length of the fence, beyond which was a rickety bridge leading in to the dark building. Adam stood watching them, his joints locked in position from the cold, two bottles of Reductil clutched in his hand. His mouth gaped open as if on the verge of throwing up. "Can I have a bang of that?" he asked the pair, who didn't even look at him.

Fiona drawled slowly, "Oh *shit*."

Donald sniggered for a while before finally speaking. "What is it?"

Fiona looked down at the papers she had finally managed to roll into a decent shape and seal with the gum from her tongue. "I forgot to put the weed in."

Donald's face screwed up, as if his centre of gravity was contained within his nose. "Oh maaan…"

"Bug!" Adam barked. "I brought your shit. Ten bucks."

Bug was clipping through the chain link fence with a pair of secateurs. "Follow me."

The other two just grumbled, picking up their stuff, Donald still whining about the joint. Adam wandered through the hole in the fence that had been stretched out, the pattern of the chain confusing his drink and perfume-addled mind.

Fiona waited for Adam to catch up. "This is fun, isn't it. It's like Mary Poppins or something." She smiled, showing a gallery of cracked, rotting teeth, the result of early-teenage bulimia, where the stomach acid brought up with her food burned the enamel off her teeth after the first few hundred times. Her figure – when in profile – still maintained that silhouette of two Ws connected to each other, a slight dip for the forehead, the nose, the slight breasts, the tiny belly protruding (which only protruded due to concave abdomen), her knees, then her Doc Martened feet.

As they disappeared inside, Adam looked back, alerted by the dull thud of wood on concrete, from multiple angles behind the fence. But he couldn't see anything for the glare of the orange streetlights on the main road some fifty feet behind. He chased after the others. "Can we just sort this out now," Adam called out, the bridge creaking with every step – a 'STOP! DANGEROUS BUILDING. DO NOT ENTER!' sign falling off the end of a metal stanchion as he ran past.

The four of them were in a concrete shell, the old work floor of the Paisley Mill, peppered with monumental pillars two grown men wouldn't be able to get their arms around. It retained the feeling of still being outside as every window had been smashed, mostly by GOMA Kids from the other side of the fence. The floor was littered with the debris of those childhood follies, rocks and bottles and deflated footballs. Bug tore around the open floor, buzzing from two Es he had taken an hour before, unsure of what to do in all the space, except to lift the tail of his jacket up his back and above his head, pretending he had a cape to fly around with. Fiona and Donald just moped around kicking the rocks on the ground. Adam leaned against one of the pillars and lit a cigarette. Bug's hand suddenly appeared over Adam's shoulder, holding two £5 notes. Adam tossed the bottles of Reductil in the air which Bug caught after spinning on the spot on his right foot.

Adam couldn't find the energy to exhale, merely breathing the

197

smoke out his nose. "I don't know what you've heard about that stuff," he said, "but don't take it with milk. You'll get brain bubbles. Some kid slipped one into his wee brother's cereal; fucker fell into his bowl of Snap Crackles, dead as a fart. So no White Russians when you're popping them. If you croak, I never knew you. Get me?"

"Space, man!" Bug screamed out, leaping around the pillars, poking Fiona and Donald in the ribs, who each stood still with their arms folded. He downed the dregs of a beer and threw the bottle as far as he could, not even reaching half down the room. The resulting smash seemed inconsequential to the decay around the high ceilings; they had seen worse than a few drunk, drugged GOMA Kids.

"Can we go yet?" Donald groaned. "This place is most definitely *not* rocking."

Fiona, who had given up and just lit the weedless joint anyway, agreed, pointing at Donald. "I concur with Doctor Donald."

Bug produced another, much larger bottle, a whisky bottle, with a handkerchief stuffed inside. "Give us yer lighter, luv," he crowed to Fiona.

"I'm outta here," Adam said, stuffing his hands in his coat pockets.

Fiona frowned. "Later potato."

Adam scuffed his feet along the black corridors: it seemed impossible to imagine the place chiming with the chatter of workers' banter from earlier that century. The emptiness of the Mill was redolent of parents' night at school, everything strangely dead with no teachers or kids running around, like something was missing; suddenly lacking its discipline and officialdom, it no longer seemed so scary.

Then, came a much louder smash then Bug's beer bottle, immediately followed by a whoosh, like a rush of wind down an alleyway. Adam turned round to see a flash of orange from the room he had just left, then three figures tearing towards him, their arms and legs windmilling around. The ceiling above Adam's head was shivering and cracking, a low pitched rumble building from where the other three were running. "Quick, the joint's gonna tumble!" Fiona cried out.

Bug trailed behind, struggling coordinate his feet – he appeared to hobbling from an injury - as the ceiling above started to fall in chalky bursts.

Adam just stared in incomprehension. "What the fuck what the fuck what the fuck…" he kept saying, his feet rooted to the spot.

Fiona and Donald ran into Adam. "What the fuck is happening!" he cried out, the sound of collapsing concrete building in volume.

"Bug's still back there," Fiona said.

Donald added, "I think he hit an old gas pipe. It just blew him right off his feet."

He was still dragging himself along, trying to stay ahead of the dust cloud, but he wasn't fast enough, and his silhouette at the end of the hallway some two hundred yards away was swallowed up by the falling ceiling, like a light colour eaten up by a darker colour on a painter's palette. He simply disappeared amongst it all.

"Bug!" Fiona screamed, Adam and Donald having to hold her back.

Adam tried to reason with her. "We can't, come on, the whole place is coming down." The rush of adrenaline left him feeling unstable, his feet turning on their sides when he ran, clutching Fiona's bony hand as they emerged out at the bridge. There was almost nothing left of the entire west wing where they had been wandering around only a minute before, and the rest of the building seemed to be giving up. Adam realised the bridge would go in a second as well if they didn't hurry.

Smoke billowed out across the River Cart, spewing out on to the deserted main road. An enormous fireball exploded as they ran across the bridge, the inertia of which sent the three teens flying over the last five yards, landing on the frosty ground, their faces golden from the fire, looking up at the destruction.

From the bushes behind them someone started clapping their hands slowly, followed by the same wooden thunking Adam had heard before crossing the bridge.

An English accent chirped from behind the fence, "Well done, sir." He and his friends were knocking their wooden canes on the pavement. "Very well done indeed!" Charles and thirty other Eton Boys stood behind them, sneaking through the hole we had made in the fence earlier. "Hold on, weren't there four of you earlier on?" he asked, looking towards Edward.

"Yes," he agreed, "there was definitely four of them going on."

Charles tutted then stifled a laugh.

The wall of fire kept burning behind, tinting everything in a warm orange haze – even the moon appeared to burn – the sky beautiful, on fire.

The flames reflected clearly in Edward's aviator sunglasses.

"Well done, Adam. You've just destroyed Paisley's most beloved landmark. What's your encore?"

All the Eton Boys broke out into laughter, heeing and hawing.

"It's just damn bad luck about that gas pipe in there," Charles said. "It could have gone at any second, but to explode when you lot were in there…well, that's just bad luck. Typical Scots bad luck." And with that they wandered off, swinging their canes and swigging from bottles of Glenmorangie.

Fiona hadn't moved since landing in the grass, catatonic with tears, her face covered by her hands.

Donald sat back resting on his palms, saying, "Fuck, man, I need a drink. I need a drink. We need to call the police or something. We need help, we need help."

Adam stood up, dusting his hands off, his voice as unmoved as ever. "I suppose I should go find a phone box and call someone. I mean…he might still be alright." Adam said it staring at the heap of rubble where Bug had been caught and he knew there was no surviving it.

"Maybe if we were living in a Jerry Bruckheimer movie," Donald sniffed, which sent Fiona into more convulsions.

She reached for the bottle of cider they had left earlier and tanked as much as her narrow throat could manage.

"They set us up," Adam said.

Donald took the bottle from Fiona and downed some, just to clear his head. "What are you talking about?"

"The taller one. It's my cousin Eddie."

"Your cousin?"

Adam smiled in defeat. "They set us up. Someone knew we were coming out here tonight. They don't just wander around like that. Paisley's not their turf, it's Glasgow."

Fiona finally managed to speak. "Wait a minute, is that those Eton Boys? The bowler hats…I've seen em tagged down Glasgow Road. Folk have been talking."

"Yeah, that's them. But they knew were coming. They must have tampered with that gas pipe or done something. They knew better than to cross the bridge, even when there was nothing stopping them. I mean, why just wait outside?"

Donald stood up. "You wasted a tenner and all."

Adam shook his head. "Nah. Bug gave me the money already."

"Could have been worse then, eh."

Adam stared back at him. "I'll go phone someone."

After an anonymous phone call at a nearby phone box, Adam detailed how he had seen "someone run into the building" and that "maybe the boy is still alive" but he "doubted it." The operator asked where he was and what his name was, upon which Adam hung up and walked quickly back towards the town centre. Fiona and Donald stayed behind, sitting on the kerb across the main road waiting for the ambulance to show up and retrieve Bug's body. She was shivering but refused Adam's coat but not the offer of six Valium ("on the house, sweetheart" Adam said). "That's the nicest thing anyone's ever done for me," she cried in gratitude.

Donald then asked for three of his own.

"You're not grieving you reprobate," Adam assured him.

The high street was deserted when Adam got there. Christmas lights hung from shop to shop across the High Street and a thirty-foot tree stood encased by a white plastic fence next to the Cenotaph.

He swallowed various pills that ranged between ten and fifteen syllables, which he had planned on selling. Events had overtaken his profit projections.

The lights were dancing all around him in a hollow manner, shapeshifting and pulverising his depression. Images of crowds of black umbrellas bullied their way into his head, flowers reading 'Marie Bernadette' brightening the vision but not his mood. He swayed down the middle of the High Street, wordless, the lights above supposed to divert attention from the empty shop fronts, all with 'To Let' or 'Quick Sale' signs hanging above their doors. The once busy department stores of the 70s and 80s now making way for £1 shops and discount baby goods to feed the mass of young mothers parading around town all day, every day, the only way they knew how to grow as people: to simply multiply themselves, to spread themselves over a thinning canvas. But those lights, Adam thought, were trying to hide that reality. He couldn't look at them anymore.

Without any more thought, he climbed a lamppost and gripped the rope keeping the lights hanging taut between the shop roofs. Even in the darkness of night they were depressingly dull. They were the same decorations the council had used as long as he could remember. Everything seemed to be encased in plastic shells, moss creeping out round the edges of the whites of Rudolph's beaming eyes.

The rope holding the lights together came away easily, and with one, hard pull he managed to tear down the whole connection, as well as the plastic Santa and reindeer heads. They buzzed on the ground off and on for a second, then the street suddenly went dark. Adam ran towards the Christmas tree, tumbling over the fence and rocking the tree back and forth out of its anchoring. It toppled forward with ease and made little sound on impact with the pavement. The angel lay in the snow amongst the broken bauble shells and reindeer heads; the entire street was decimated: the strings connecting the lights were all snapped, so they dangled uselessly between the shops, as if they were the only mechanism keeping the buildings upright, and he turned the rubbish bins upside down and kicked and spread out the litter over the street.

Adam paused for breath in the cold night air. He inhaled deeply. "It feels good to be outside again," he said.

Chapter Twenty-three
'Baby, I must be wasted'

The flat was all blinking neon eyes when Adam got home; another message on his answering machine, the television on standby, but faltering after years of abuse. His light box sat flickering on the floor in the corner of the room, like a wicked child. He sat on the edge of the sofa, head in his hands; the sounds from down on the street refused to desist, a strangulating air bearing down from each corner of the room. The flat had turned on him now: its past ease was sufficient enough to allow him to navigate every room in pitch darkness if need be, but it now felt alien, sitting, leaning forward as if waiting for the brakes to be hit on a bus, and then, relief of backwards momentum, and kinetic equilibrium. But the relief never came. He was stuck, suspended indefinitely, his head always a pace ahead of his body, extra Gs inflicted on my troubled brain. He jumped up and stabbed the play button on the answering machine, hoping to hear his dad's voice.

"Message One - Hello Mr McNee? This is Market Research calling, we were just wondering if you would like to participate in our survey..."

There wasn't any point in letting the message finish. Without unplugging the machine, he picked it up and threw it across the room. It had felt much lighter in his hand than expected, so when it met the wall it didn't quite crumble satisfactorily. The sound of broken electrics and whimpering followed. "Shut up, shut up, shut the FUCK up!" he screamed towards the window, the noise now growing despite the late hour. This was indeed the hour of the street – the street's revenge. A man ambled drunkenly below, muttering obscenities and waving fists to imaginary adversaries. It seemed so unnecessary; Adam fetched a glass of water to throw on him, but he was already away by the time Adam got back, glass in hand.

A cloud of thin smoke rose up from the mangled circuitry and all Adam could see was Bug's crumpled corpse. He craved to hear one of Bug's monosyllabic remarks again; to see one of his and Fiona's sloppy kisses. Just then the phone started ringing. He grabbed for it.

"Yes, yes, I'm here."

"Eh…hello, this is Malcolm McDonald. Is that Mr McNee?"

Adam sighed, "No, it's the wrong number."

"Oh right, I'm sorry to bother you sir—"

"Well no, you can stay and chat if you want, I mean, I'm not doing anything."

There was a long pause at the other end. "Th…that's OK…I've got to…um," then the phone clicked off and Adam threw it down dejectedly.

Vodka then whisky, then some confused looks as twenty-four hour news played with constant weather updates, their sad and trite segues from the preceding story so painful as to kick-start Adam's nausea again. It felt like hours passed, just staring blankly at the 'breaking news' and 'news updates' and soap opera punditry and entertainment news and Israel was still a mess and the reporters insisted on wearing bullet-proof vests and running to the front lines liberating entire African villages with nothing but a wireless videophone and a dramatic pause before saying their name and where they were embedded and another reporter stood on a melting glacier and said the sun would boil everyone to death in about a thousand years and India was going to overtake America as the world's leading polluter (there's that argument gone then) and we were still arming countries then declaring war on them then sending them aid then demanding an end to the genocide and then realising it was performed by us and Noam Chomsky still thought every country was fascist even if they had a free press and a democratically elected government (every country is shit!) and they interviewed Christopher Hitchens and he made a reference to Thomas Paine who Adam would have been studying at university if Bob hadn't killed himself and a poll suggested the general public would support a return to capital punishment and the flogging of illegal immigrants and there was going to be another policy announcement at lunchtime next day but the political editors already knew what it was and had already dismissed it as shallow spin doctoring before the announcement was even made (the joy!) and everything was for sale to the lowest bidder with Cabinet connections and passports were being hawked by Ministers and Adam passed out for a few hours and a woman's shrieking laughter woke him up, the one that did the breakfast programme and wore too much makeup (*she can't be that ugly first thing?* Adam thought) causing her co-anchor, every time he turned to her, to give a tiny jump on their beige sofa and Adam fixed another drink and a joint and a sleep for a while and he forgot to call in sick for work and none of it mattered anymore. It was all a long time ago.

Chapter Twenty-four

'Ciderdreams'

A Big Issue seller was singing Christmas Carols outside the entrance of the frozen foods shop. His hat on the ground brimmed with pound coins, none of the copper dreck. Love was truly there in Paisley.

It was a weekday, so Freezo-foods was packed; the Two-Meals-for-£2 cabinet was already half empty. The store was almost completely silent, save for the occasional squeak of trolleys and the rustling of iced-up own-brand food packets, feeling the heft, examining prices, no point getting ripped aft. People stared down into long rows of freezer cabinets lining the aisles like glass coffins, inspecting the frozen and the dead. Everything was merchandised with red and white stripes, which, when seen as a collective, proved migraine-inducing. Fat mothers jammed the aisles with their double-berth prams, the fat grandmothers (walking stick in each hand) waddled behind in their dark blue anoraks, shoulders showered liberally with dandruff, and each with the same mysterious dark stain down the front. All the other customers: good and proper drunks like Adam: shabby and run down looking, ruffled hair, long coats, ill-fitting trousers – and just as eager to escape attention.

At the front of the store was a small newspaper stand with a collection of the local rags. At the back Adam found an old one, the Weekly Feast. It read: "LOCAL LANDMARK COLLAPSES," then in the subheading below, "VANDALS DESTROY CHRISTMAS DECORATIONS/SPIRIT."

A security guard started following Adam's staggering path around the aisles. A light whirring noise started above him – the black

209

ball that concealed the security cameras roaming up and down on its rail. He stood there, staring lifelessly into the freezer cabinets – 2-for-£2 or 3-for-£1.50. Life is all about choices.

The guard walked past him, so close Adam could smell him: cigarettes and too many stale cheap machine coffees. A cold sweat was starting to seep through the front of Adam's blue linen shirt. His hands were shaking violently as he filled his trolley with microwave meals-for-one, then he completely lost control of his limbs and flopped down to his knees. He pulled himself up by one of the freezer door handles, choking, gasping in nervous hysterics until he made it to the alcohol aisle. There was a special offer on Totov vodka at £5, plus it was in a 'buy-one-get-one-free'. "You'd almost think the shops want us to be lazy slothful alcoholics," Adam said half laughing, half crying to a drunk-looking man in his thirties as he packed out his trolley.

They both reached for the last one but he let Adam have it. "You look like you need it more than me," the man said, pulling at the dark rings under his eyes.

Adam placed his bottles down carefully on the conveyer belt, followed lastly by his sad little family of microwave meals, brother and sister-curries, cousin-pasta bakes, emancipated together from their frozen refugee camp. The checkout girl – bored, bad acne – scanned everything through, chewing gum methodically, never lifting her gaze from the till screen, her security that kept her from having to deal with any humans.

"£23.99," she said simply, ciderdreams passing behind her sunken pupils. She rammed Adam's things into three translucent red and white striped bags, all ready for the outside world to judge.

Adam dropped his receipt as he turned away, and as he knelt down to pick it up the blood rushed to his head. His eyes drowned in black and when they cleared a figure was standing over him, totally engulfed in flames. Adam backed up against the wall.

"Is this yours, son?" It was the security guard.

Adam took it from him, choking back violent coughs.

Outside, he held the bags with the logo facing the inside of his leg but he could do nothing to hide the red and white stripes that screamed 'discount' and 'failure'. A packed bus passed him and he could feel the collective stare out the window; that recognition from the women shoppers and their golden perms, and the majesty of their blue, fabric Marks and Spencer bags. All the bottles were clear to see. *Where's his food? He's not going home to drink at this time, is he? On a weekday? Why's he not at school?*

Chapter Twenty-five
'A Sense Of Freedom'

A indignant mob stood huddled around the front doors of Fix It, ankle-high slush spraying around them as the car park filled up. He could hear them from inside, rattling the shutters, demanding entry, satisfaction. When the shutters rose they filed in, clutching their faulty goods, receipts already outstretched, ready for return, refund. That was the way now. The inadequacy of everything. They knew what their goddamn entitled to. People suddenly become lawyers when required to return products to shops: "I know my rights!"

The putrid smell of raw sewage permeated the shop floor that morning. Jim explained to Adam: "the nightshift clogged up the toilets. Ope, yes, bust a main under the building, so it did."

Adam replied, "So, we can honestly say we work in shit?"

Cheryl lifted her glance from her pocket mirror, noticing Adam slouched over his till. "Where have you been? Sheila's been going mental. She hates people being late."

Adam's morning whisky had gone straight to his spinal cord, making any slight movement strenuous. "I had a sore throat. But don't worry, I've got plenty of medicine." He tapped his pocket containing a valium, ketamine and some miniature whiskies. "They're going to sack me anyway. Gross misconduct. I didn't see anything gross about it apart from Cameron Marshall's overgrown nose hair."

Paul dumped some timber down in front of Cheryl's desk - always the caveman. He had a small cut above his right eyebrow and was muttering something about "Fucking pigeons…"

Cheryl tutted. "Don't you ever stop swearing?"

"I thought you liked it dirty?" he leered, grabbing her from across the desk, wrapping his arms around her delicate hips and lifting her up with ease, those savage triceps of his winning the day again.

Adam wasn't so much watching them as wishing, like any desperate drunk does to couples in bars, wishing he was in the man's position, being held, being loved, being argued with. That was the real joy: those petty, regular troubles of The Couple; the sheer simplicity of their joy. Day in, day out relations, sex.

His spell was broken by a fat, tattooed man knocking his hand on the till top. His fat wife stood silently next to him, head bowed solemnly. The man's sleeves were pushed up past his forearms, where a tattoo on his left arm showed a rose with 'Mum RIP' written inside the scroll. On his right arm it said, 'Yvonne Luv 4eva'.

Adam gestured at the man's arm. "Did they charge by the letter or something?"

The man didn't understand. "Wissat smell?" he asked, as a large queue quickly built behind him as he fumbled with his change. The wife stepped in to help but he pushed her back with a well-applied arm. "Just gonnae stan back wuman? Am handlin' it."

She retreated accordingly, just like a well trained dog would. Adam didn't break his gaze from the woman's face during the whole transaction, mouth hanging open, eyes dead with pity – this poor mess of a woman, he thought, *is that really the best he can do for you? A fucking tattoo on his arm?* Adam supposed that was the closest the man would come to showing affection. Her sleeve rode up as she wiped her face: whiting self-harm slash scars bubbled on the surface of her arm, probably long hidden from his uncaring gaze, whenever

214

they undressed in the safe darkness of the bedroom. Adam imagined her lying blankly in bed, staring up at the ceiling, as the man forced his way inside her with his half-limp member (excessive consumption of saturated fats causes impotence), his fuzzy belly riding on top of her, damp with sweat – the same desire and consideration as he would give to slamming the microwave door shut. She would tell him, 'Slow down. You're going too hard.' He would tell her, 'Shut up, I'll be done in a second.' He had been down the pub most of the night, flirting with barmaids that humour them for tips. He would stumble in, stinking of curry, masturbation and sick, with tales from the Post Office depot: 'they've got this fuckin Paki working wey us noo.' His fat, stunted penis would already be crusted white from jacking off in the pub toilets with thoughts of the birds from the Carling Lager adverts between the fitba.

She wore the look of hidden bottles of Valium in the bedroom drawer; of sneaking drinks from the half bottle of gin from the bathroom medicine cabinet after cleaning his pubic hair and dirt out of the bath; of cutting herself with her husband's razor because there was nothing else for her to do, nowhere else to go. Just a little sign of blood might remind her she used to be alive. Still bleeding, still breathing.

Paul was in the Smoker's Room with Cheryl, pointing at the cut above his eyebrow, still explaining how a pigeon attacked him on his way into the shop. She was coughing but trying to hide it - clearly irritated by his smoking. He had left the door open and the smoke was now drifting into the canteen. Adam poured himself a miniature whisky into a brown plastic coffee cup and stared at the white wall in front of him. Minutes later Paul and Cheryl were arguing and she stormed out into the canteen, slamming the Smoker's Room door behind her. She hauled out a chair next to Adam and threw herself down, his whisky lapping up and over the edge of the cup. They sat in silence for a few minutes then she switched on the TV and continually flicked channels.

"Can you turn that off, please?" Adam asked after the fourth circuit of the four channels they could actually receive. "I feel…odd."

Cheryl crossed her arms, rifling them under her armpits. "It's just a rumour about Paul and this slut in Finance. Right?"

"I…I couldn't say." He was lying. Everyone had heard the rumours. The not-so-secret phone calls. The video making its way around the security guards (they got it two days at a time).

She edged her chair nearer him, pushing her hair behind her ear to give him a clearer look at her face. Adam had never seen her eyes so close up before, and it was only from such close proximity that he saw her desperation, the desperation he saw everywhere: that terror of being alone in this, the Great Modern World. It was obvious that Cheryl tried men like people try shoes, flitting from pair to pair until you find one that fits just so. Fortunately Adam's shoes came in bottles and powder form.

The air between them was already hesitant. The energy from her hands was tangible, resting on the table, her fingertips flickering for contact, ready to bridge the short distance to his. She stared at him, almost pleading, in silence; she couldn't do it all herself, her eyes told him, but he was useless to her, she just didn't know it then. At the moment, in the heat of her argument with Paul, she had looked in to the empty canteen and saw Adam sitting there that it all made sense to her. Someone just had to find the heart to tell her she was mistaken.

Adam got up and left without saying a word, Cheryl's hands still on the table, still hoping that he might come back and fix her, mend her.

In the toilets, Adam took out his small plastic sandwich bag of ketamine. He tapped some out on top of the cistern and snorted several lines. It was far too much to handle in public but the self-harming woman's face had rubbed him up the wrong way. It had compounded some thoughts gestating in him since an incident upon coming to work that morning: It was before dawn, first light still but a far-off dream. A car had slowed down as it approached him, a group of blokes still partying from the night before, inside. One of them leaned out an open window to shout 'hey, dickhead!' at him. Adam stopped dead in his tracks as the car sped off, the window quickly going back up to bottle in their laughter. *What have I done to upset them so much?* he wondered. That was when he realised, as he looked up at the sky, tears already forming in his eyes, as the light of morning stars which had made their way across the universe for millions of years, only to come resting on him: it was because he existed, because he happened to be there on that street at that particular time and place. And he was no good to them.

He looked at myself in the mirror, took a swig of whisky and batted his tears down. Luckily, he had remembered to bring the bottle of White Light with him – or what remained of it - kept safe in his red apron, ready when needed. He sucked in its sweet scent and felt the drip of the ketamine already working on him. It was only a matter of time now…

The shop had lulled, so he swallowed a Valium, not even bothering to hide the fact anymore - he also added four miniatures to his apron, which was now a brimming, mobile chemical plant.

"What's that you're eating, Adam?" asked Jim.

"Just a…mint."

"Could I have one?"

"That's…not a good idea."

Customers asked him where things were, but he just barked out random aisle numbers.

"Where's the paint?" shouted some figure in a blue cagoule. Faces weren't registering anymore.

"The paint's located in the eternal fire burning in our souls, the one that transcends space and time, even history. It's beautiful. You should go look," he said deadpan, "Then again, I stare at a door that says 'No Exit' for six hours, so what do I know?"

He guzzled more Valium – this time to calm myself. It felt like his head was being slowly decompressed – all around him there was noise, loud unnecessary noise: children crying because they wanted to go home; electric cleaning buggies zooming past then beeping as they went into reverse; and tannoy announcements for managers every ten seconds because someone wanted to complain.

Then suddenly, it all stopped. Everyone seemed to move in slow motion and the music playing above could be heard crystal clear – Talking Heads, 'Once in a Lifetime'. A family walked past with a trolley-full of Christmas lights and decorations. All of them holding hands. "Wow. Look at that," Adam said slowly, in monotone, sniffing from the bottle of White Light. Nicola appeared, far away at the end of the shop, looking towards him, the only thing in focus, then blurring out again.

The rain was bouncing off the pavement and for a few hours Angus and Adam went quietly about their work, dragging in the abandoned trolleys, but Adam's brain was shutting down: He had started to walk into oncoming traffic with complete disregard. A blonde girl tore her way through the car park in a Volkswagen Golf Coupe, whilst talking on her mobile phone. Adam stepped out in front of her and she slammed on her brakes just in time. She blasted her horn then yelled, "Hey! I almost ran you over, you clown!"

"Yeah, I know," Adam said nonchalantly.

"I mean…I could've killed you!"

"You *are* right." He paused. "Do you want to try again?" He lay down on the road ready for her. She had to drive up onto the kerb to get past him.

Mark was wandering over in some crazed-looking stupor, carrying a Burger King bag and a bottle of Totov.

Adam got up off the road. "Mark! Mark! Over here."

He stumbled over, tripping up on the kerb in front of Adam. "Whoops, who put that there?" he asked himself then laughed. "Hey. Like…what are you doing down there, man?"

"Mark. You're fucking wasted."

"Of course!" he said triumphantly and swigged from the bottle.

"Hey, so are you, man."

"You know it. Fuckers are gonna sack me. Taking the piss out Spencer other day."

They sat down on a secluded kerb – hidden from the CCTV – and shared the bottle for an hour or so.

Mark said, "Someone ratted me out about till pinching." He dismissed Adam before he had a chance to deny it. "I know it wasn't you. It doesn't matter. I'm just enjoying my last paid lunch, then I'm out of here."

"What are you going to do?" Adam asked.

"Go out in style. You might as well join me seeing as we're both on the way out." Mark handed him the Totov and strutted back inside, buzzing with vodka-confidence. He took Jim's headset from the front desk and dialled for the tannoy. There was a 'ping-pong' from above, and Adam watched the sky, ready for it to fall. Mark cleared his throat and said as politely as possible, "This a customer announcement…"

Sheila poked her head out her first floor office to see what was going on.

Then Mark screamed, "…would all customers please fuck off home!" and took off, running through the aisles as security came streaming out their office, still clutching their sandwiches, pornos lying open on their desk.

Adam grabbed a radio and chased after Mark.

Jim saluted them on the way past. "Ope, yes, very well, good luck, soldiers!"

The guards gave chase, darting in and out the wrong aisles, but by the time the camera guards had told the ones on the ground where to go, they were gone again, off screaming with laughter, singing over the tannoy.

All the customers stopped in the aisles looking up at the tannoy speakers in disbelief.

Mark took gasping breaths between each word: "Let the record show that Sheila Walsh regularly steals money from petty cash. The reason I know this is because I walked in on her in the counting room one day. She then threatened to expose me as a thief, which, incidentally, I am."

Then there was the sound of a struggle as the guards finally caught up with him – Mark gargling his last few swear words and threats of violence through the tannoy: "One last thing: I saw you Adam. I saw you and Nicola that night, and Trent's going to know too…"

Then there was quiet again. Everyone's attention turned to Mark, being ushered quickly away by security to their holding room upstairs. The police would get there when they could: when they could be arsed. Adam looked around, expecting to see Trent rushing for him, but people went back to pushing their trolleys around, the show over; and him, the lost boy holding the bottle of vodka in the power tools aisle. His stomach was quivering. It was over: Nicola, the GOMA Kids, Fix It, Scotland.

This, he knew, was the time to act. He would go screaming around the aisles, raging at the lack of compassion, the denial of humanity in favour of value for money. The replacement of real emotion with laminate shelving. Self-assemble furniture was their new sex. He was going to show them, alright! He would empty racks of timber over Paul for cheating on Cheryl so brazenly; tell Sheila what he really thought of her, and he knew what she did when she got back to that empty house of hers every night: she cried and drank and watched television and bought lottery tickets because someone had to win it (and why not her? Why not anyone?) and her blood boiled when soap opera characters she hated came on screen and when adverts reminded her how ugly and fat she was. Yes, he knew Sheila pretty well. He would take control of the tannoy like Mark, and everyone would listen. Boy, they would listen! (Adam walked slowly towards the tills, nursing more of Mark's Totov down my neck, the plan in his head all worked out now. "Goodbye Jim," Adam said as he passed him.) He kept his head down and imagined if he still had his apron, he would throw it down and stamp on it in front of everybody, just to let everyone know the chronic injustice he had suffered!

Sheila grabbed him from behind. "What the hell do you think you're doing? You're blind drunk!"

Adam looked ahead at the front door, the white letters 'No Exit' distorted and doubled, when something like a recurring piano motif started playing in his head, later sprinkled with a light string section for emotion – with a lilt in his voice, he said to her, "I'm in love with someone, don't you know. Love is here. Love has come for me."

She looked back down at her logbooks and said, "Leave your apron on the desk." But Adam just kept walking out, out through the car park drinking heavily from his bottle of vodka, darting in and out of traffic until he was as far as the Scottish flag, next to the modern art piece at the main entrance. Waiting for a break in the traffic, he ran across the five lane roundabout to the centre island, cars honking and blasting their horns at him. He was just so drawn to the flag flapping about. A strong wind swept past Fix It, in off the banks of the River Clyde – Adam had never noticed its serenity before. The wind skirted it, like ghosts dancing, dipping their toes in ever so slightly, causing tiny rifts in the river surface.

The vodka had gone right through him, so he undid his flies and started pissing against the turd-shaped metal statue, looking up and winking at the flag as he did so.

In my brief time at Fix It, the Saltire had faded even more distinctly, almost to the point of whitewash. With the wind blowing so strongly in his face – a very real sense of freedom now – he felt compelled to bellow out a sarcastic 'O Flower of Scotland' at the top of his voice. Some drunks sat by the river joined in, but they all forgot the words after the first verse. They tried to start it up again, but gave up. So Adam did up his flies and went home. He had never felt like much of a patriot. How can you, when you don't even feel part of this world? It's just reductionism. Why not go further and feel patriotism for your county, your street, your house, your living room, you head. You couldn't feel a part of any of those things.

Outside the off-licence a solitary boy on his bike circled around the upright sign out front: 'The cost of boozing just keeps falling'. Adam banged on the glass door with the side of his fist.

"Hello?" he called out. "Sammy, it's Adam, open up!" He looked at the opening hours in the window. "It's 9am. He should be open by now," he explained to the boy who wasn't really listening.

The boy said to him, "You'll no get in there, pal. S'shut."

Adam arched his hands over his eyes to see inside.

"Got any fags, pal?" the boy asked.

He looked at the boy, realising how young he was. "No," he answered distractedly.

"Prick," the boy muttered, riding off.

Now Adam realised there was police tape around the open cash register, and dark purple stains on the floor that looked like wine or dried blood; the crime scene frozen in time. So he returned home empty-handed, spirits running low.

Chapter Twenty-six
'Another ruckus'

The light box had been flickered on and off all night against the bedroom wall, filling the room with light, then emptying, filling the room, then emptying. The pigeons in the roof above cooed with satisfaction at their lot, each tiny movement of the family reverberating round the rafters, flapping and shuffling, together, together. They just had to shout about it. Eventually Adam fell into a Detractyl-induced hallucination, as the early evening sunlight struggled through the curtains into an almost impenetrably dense cloud of cannabis smoke hanging in the air; chalky remnants of the ketamine he had been snorting were sprayed across the coffee table; any attempts to ignore the diabolical depravity of the situation couldn't escape him. The carpet was but an ashtray, like the floor of a quarry, rubble and ash working its way into the pile.

The bottle of White Light was in his hand, held close to his face, because if the smell relented for even a second he would immediately start sobbing into the arm rest of the sofa, which was now stained dark with tears. As soon as any sound from the pigeons started above him, he recoiled, rolling around in the foetal position, clasping his hands over his ears, or yelling, just to hide their contentedness.

Eventually it became too much: he screamed a final warning at them, which they ignored, of course. He grabbed a broom from the kitchen and threw the window open, the setting sun burning orange straight through his eyes. The cannabis smoke cloud gushed out in waves. He started banging on the ceiling with the broom handle – small puffs of plaster falling on to my face – and shouting, "Rouse!

Rouse! Rouse!"

After some frenzied flapping about in the rafters, they flew out from under the gutter one by one, straight into the direction of the sun, free as kisses. He threw the broom down dejectedly and cursed himself that they might not come back.

So it was with a heavy heart that he walked the streets of Glasgow that night, the quiet in the flat had unsettled him to alcoholic fracture. No matter, the streets were all a mess: Fat, bloated, drunken women cavorting with a taxi driver at the rank, trying to get a free fare as his mate whistled the EastEnders theme tune as he stared at Page 3 of The Sun; gangs in tracksuits still stalking the streets with bottles of Buckfast and kicking in phone booth doors and shop shutters, shouting at strangers just trying to get a fuckin rise, man.

The buildings appeared to be made of rubber, the roofs bending, arching out over the streets, mouths open, ready to consume everything.

On Sauchiehall Street Adam took some money out a cash machine – his account drained to only £10.07 left, just enough to take out a whole tenner.

Nicola stood at the bar in Nice 'N Sleazy's, which was crammed almost to capacity, collectively booing as someone put on Jeff Buckley's 'Lover, You Should Have Come Over' on the jukebox, ruining the atmosphere. Nicola had on a long flowing skirt, less flashy, but more sensual with a beautiful bright red lipstick, like she had kissed a knife.

"How are you?" When she kissed him on the cheek he felt the

thickness of her lipstick stick to his skin for a second as she pulled back.

He hesitated. A cold sweat clung to his forehead and palms. A feeling of absolute terror had stifled him all day since Freezo-foods, the wires in his brain had finally been fried. In his reflection behind the bar, he didn't recognise himself; he looked down at his hands and wondered whose they were. Behind those sunken eyes, he wondered what thoughts permeated his brain? He sure as hell don't know.

"I was so worried," she said. "But Trent said not to call you in case the police were there."

"Is that right…"

She paused. "Trent told me about Bug and everything else that happened. Donald's been pretty intense since then, sleeping on Trent's sofa and stuff."

Adam said nothing.

"Your work's been calling me, Adam. They said you've missed three shifts in the last four days. What's going on? Where've you been?"

Shit, four days. Is that all? "Drinking, I suppose. I put you down as my emergency contact."

She took his hand and guided him round the room in search of a table but nothing could lift the nightmarish visions he was having. All around them were rampaging hordes of alcopop disciples raising their glasses in hollow toasts. Cheering and laughing and shouting and screaming then spewing and fucking and sucking then wiping then sleeping.

A table all dressed in black were desperately conferring with

227

each other about something and looking at me with a strange intrigue. "I'm telling you, it's not her," one murmured. Then all five of them got out their seats at once.

"Here you go, Nicola," they said.

"Put in a good word for us with Trent will you?" said another pulling chairs out for them. The group left to stand at the crowded bar.

Adam clutched his temples, pressing them down, down, his laughter bordering on hysterical.

Nicola said, "I got you some scented candles. You know, to help you sleep." She passed him a small Superdrug bag with two red candles inside.

"Thanks, I'll give them a try," he said, sniffing them.

She eyed him worriedly. "So…I saw the newspapers."

He nodded, impressed. "That the end of the small talk then? Wasn't meant to happen that way? Thought we were going to die in there? Haha! Fire is just so hot. Concrete so heavy. And they knew we were coming."

"Adam. You're rambling."

He rubbed his face, dragging his eyelids down to his substantial cheekbones.

"And you're drunk."

"Don't defend him!" Adam said, raising his voice. "You weren't there."

"Defend who?"

"You know who."

"Christ, it's Trent isn't it? He's more of a father than a boyfriend, Adam."

He lit one of the scented candles and held it in his hand, babbling incoherently into the flame, passing his hand back and forth over it.

She blew it out.

"Fuck, Nicola!" Adam said, lighting a cigarette. "I want out of all this. This bullshit!"

She reached for his hand. "You're just scared. I would be too—"

"No!" He slammed his hand down on the table, startling the people next to them. "It's not fear. Can't you see? It's too late for that. He knows, Trent knows. Mark saw us, he told the entire store."

The front doors flew open, crashing against the wall, switching the jukebox off like a broken record. Three Eton Boys stood in the doorway, in their bowler hats and brandishing their canes as always.

Charles shouted out, "Sorry about the ruckus!" and the broken record sound stopped – the frantic beat of The Buzzcocks 'Ever Fallen in Love' starting up and people sprung to their feet to dance. He was sporting a bizarre fake handlebar moustache. Eddie joined him, with a third companion Adam recognised from the Old Mill incident.

"Sorry about the ruckus, Adam," Charles repeated as he stood over their table.

"What...do you want," he asked slowly. "Cos if you want raise hell right here and get us *all* arrested then be my guest."

"No, that won't be necessary." He twirled his cane round in his hand and pulled up a chair along with Edward.

"That won't be necessary," added the third man.

Charles looked slightly embarrassed and said out the corner of his mouth, "Yes, Nigel, I've said that already."

Eddie smirked, "Always a pleasure, Adam."

"Fuck you, Eddie," Adam said casually, not even looking at him.

Charles straightened the lapels of his suit jacket and shouted to the door, "Will somebody shut that door already, it's bloody *Baltic* in here!"

Charles offered his hand.

"Fuck...*off*!" Adam swatted his hand away viciously.

"What's going on, Adam?" asked Nicola.

"I haven't a clue. I really don't."

"We've come into some information that might interest you, Adam," Charles said, stroking his moustache thoughtfully, only for it to fall off. "Drat. Ah, it spoils the illusion now. Oh well." He turned to Nicola. "I especially know it will interest *you*."

She tucked her hair behind her ear, nervously.

Adam said, "Charles, please just fuck off."

"Well, I never! Nigel, cover your ears!" He lowered his voice, "what a dirty, dirty mouth you have, mister. Somebody should wash that out for you. Wire brush and dental, I think. Yes, indeed."

Someone blew cigarette smoke in his direction, causing him to stand up and brushed around the shoulders of his suit. He gradually raised his voice, "A pity about the fucking *proles* in here." He ushered Nigel to go and wait outside.

"I've heard enough of this bollocks. Come on, Nicola, we're going," Adam said, pushing his chair back.

Charles laid his cane across Adam's chest. "So, you don't want to hear my proposition?"

Nicola was increasingly panicked to get out. "Let's go, Adam, this is all bullshit."

"I assure you it's not," Charles smirked.

"What, then?" Adam slurred.

Charles began twirling his cane, unaware of the person next to him that he kept striking. "This won't end happily, Adam, you do know that don't you?" He bent down to speak into his ear. "My offer is this: tell Trent to leave town or we'll make your life unliveable."

Adam stared back at him, the comedy of what he had been threatened with lost on Charles. "Unliveable." He broke into hysterical laughter, leaning down between his knees.

"Is he alright?" Charles asked Nicola, motioning with a spinning finger that Adam had lost his mind. "Could you get lost for a second, darling?" He tossed some loose change on the floor. "There, go get yourself a treat."

Adam composed himself and said to Nicola. "Maybe it's best you go."

She gripped his hand then departed.

Edward hissed, "You're such a gent, Adam. I wish I was so inclined..."

"It's easy," Charles said. "Adam was raised properly, right, Eddie?"

Edward said, "I wouldn't be too sure. Father's a bit of a peasant."

"Anyway," Charles said, "this wasn't our making. We want you to understand that. We came to tell you about something. It involves this." He slid a handkerchief with the letters E.B. on it, wrapped around   something.

Inside the handkerchief was a gun. Adam smirked when he unwrapped it. "Is that real?"

"Yes," Charles laughed. "It's real. Honest to God."

Adam pulled the trigger, and a red piece of fabric with the words 'BANG!' written on it shot out.

Charles clapped his hands in joy. "Oh, that was terrific!"

"That's a hell of a piece. Look, what do you want to tell me?"

"I think you already know."

Eddie placed his bowler hat down on the table. "He's been fucking her the whole time." He nodded at Nicola standing at the bar. "We know you know. You're not that stupid."

Adam finished his cigarette and immediately lit another.

Eddie said, "She's making a cuckold of you. She's breaking your rusty little heart."

Charles shook his head gravely. "It makes us terribly sad for all this to come out in such a public place."

The jukebox changed to Joy Division's 'Atmosphere', the bass rumbling so loud, Adam's empty glass fell off the edge of the table.

Charles picked his hat up. "Just something to think about next time you see Trent. That is if he doesn't see you first. I hope he doesn't find out about you two carrying on behind his back. If I were you I would get him first."

Adam snatched Charles's hat from his hands. "It know Mark has been creeping around for you guys. He'll do anything for some pills."

Edward snapped his finger at Adam. "He's a smart one, is this."

Charles grabbed his hat back with an angrier than usual, "Sorry about the ruckus! Come *on*, Nigel!" Then they slammed the doors shut behind them.

Chapter Twenty-seven

'Cat'

The gates leading up to Cat's house flapped wide open in the wind, the house inside bathed in a strange orange hue, as if lit from the floors up, curtains blowing out open windows on every floor. Adam trudged heavy footsteps, dragging his way through the thick gravel, the sound of 'All Tomorrow's Parties' by The Velvet Underground blasting from the hi-fi, secreting out every window and the open front door. He stepped into the mess of clothes dumped around the hallway, all the way up the staircase, a Scottish saltire dangling from the chandelier in the centre of everything. Cat had stripped the paintings lining the staircase leaving gaping holes between the frames, which she had filled with spray painted slogans like 'Only god is laughing' and 'All I ever wanted was to make someone happy'. Lamps were overturned on the floor but still on; empty bottles of Lambrini and Reductil sat on the bottom stair.

"Cat, you in?" Adam called out.

There was a gentle sobbing from the top landing, where Cat was sitting with her knees pulled up to her chest. As he ascended the stairs towards her she made the decision to slide her arms under her legs.

"What's going on, Cat?" The stairs felt unsure under his feet, like climbing a stationary escalator: he kept expecting motion.

Cat's words fought through the thick air, desperate to get out. Even she didn't know how many pills she had taken, but her speech was languid and slurred. "I had the photo shoot for the magazine today," she said, slowly drawing her arms out. They were in pieces, slashed with razors, words like 'ZERO' and 'ALONE' carved into the delicate skin on the inside of her arms, destroyed forever. "They say it's some of their best photos, yet," she said proudly. "I was feeling a bit nervous, so they gave me some nice pills and did the hard work for me. Being a writer's just like heaven, don't you know."

"So I see." Adam fell down on the stair below her and reached for her hand.

"They say if this doesn't crack me on the London scene, nothing will. I'm going to be a star, Adam." She shook his fingers (now gone limp) reassuringly, positive of her bloody victory. She was still holding some of the brown bottles they had given her. Someone at the magazine had actually got a pharmacist to prescribe them. "They say it might knock me sideways for a few weeks as long as I get to a hospital in time. That should give the magazine's PR long enough to start rumours of my demise."

Adam was speaking just as languid, with no hint of urgency. "Cat, these could kill you."

"What was it they said? You could get killed by a bus tomorrow and what would you have to show for it?"

"You don't walk out in front of buses, though, do you Cat?"

She carried the collective tragedy of what they as a generation were trying to achieve: they didn't know. So maybe pills would work. Perhaps some powder instead. Or fucking a stranger might help.

Her eyes were love itself, caged, locked up in a jar, desperate to escape, by embrace or kiss, it didn't matter, as long as someone else was there. And there she was sitting on a ridiculously wide staircase surrounded by a United Nations of antiques from countries she had only ever been shown photos of from her father's business travels, crying on to the shoulder of someone who was now as much a stranger as that very father. So many times she had asked him to look after her. Adam remembered when in school they skipped classes for a day to take Ecstasy in the park. They ran around in the sun, coming up together, letting their shirt tails hang out, blowing in the wind, jumping into the tadpole pond. They danced for hours to the music of screaming children and the coming traffic of commuters. And they climbed trees. When they reached the top they stretched their arms up to the sky, reaching out miles above them. Then evening came and they started to come down. The dark was getting to Cat and she was afraid she would be left alone to deal with something she wasn't ready for. They fell asleep in a single sleeping bag on the study room floor, stacks of her father's law books towering around them. She was shivering and pulled his arm across her chest. Sitting below her on the staircase that night, he kept seeing her face turning towards him – as it had on the roundabout that summer's day – a smile stretching out across her face, her eyes wandering down and away. That two second movie clip looped in repeat, in slow motion, contracting in on itself, becoming infinite, like a pair of mirrors facing each other.

Adam handed her a bottle of Totov. "You might as well keep drinking til you throw those pills up."

She turned the bottle up, facing the saltire on the chandelier, and took in what she could. "I remember," she slurred, "how much my dad loved me."

"Where is he?"

"He's not here. No one is. They're all at Arthur's poetry reading at the Drunken Spastic. Getting high on his *imagery*. Loaded on his *metaphors*. So I thought I would try a metaphor of my own."

"And this is it?" he asked, looking at her arms.

"Yes."

"And what does it mean?"

She stared at him and started to cry – in frustration, not sadness. "I don't know. The magazine never told me."

Adam came up a step to let her fall against his shoulder, and like a little boy full of wonder at the vast scale of the world, the first time he had ever seen a globe, he said, "I'm just so drunk."

And that was how they sat for hours until Cat fell asleep. Adam tried in vain to find a blanket, but all the beds had been stripped, so he pulled the saltire down from the chandelier and wrapped it around Cat.

With rest of the house empty, he wandered freely around the ground floor where ashtrays had been thrown around, furniture overturned, photos were turned around to face the wall. All but one photo remained in place, a photo of herself from her prom which Adam only recognised from the dress; she had scratched her face out. Adam put the photo in his pocket, knowing it would only upset her if she saw it. Plus he wanted something to remember her by.

The kitchen was a sorry mess of stained whisky and wine glasses, the rims all caked in the same red lipstick as if from the same night. The fridge contained only expired tins of fruit and empty bottles of vodka mistakenly put back inside. A Post-It note on the door said, "See you soon, Cat. Luv you." It could have been from anyone, anytime, any place. And the deliberate misspelling of 'love' seemed trite to Adam. Colloquialisms of love. The handwriting was nothing but a few scratches of ink, written in a hurry no doubt, possibly in the dark, which led Adam to think it was from her father, dipping back into the household in the middle of the night, and this was all he could do for her now. What was it with fathers?

Adam took a seat on Cat's father's leather chair and lit a cigar from the counter beside, sipping a glass of malt whisky until the sun came up, trundling home in the puffy snow, sharing the streets, as you do at that time of the morning, with milkmen, returning night shift workers, and failed lovers.

He sat in his living room tears falling down his face, the television screen staring back at him, muddied, an indistinct blur. His arms dripped uselessly by his sides, too paralysed by pills to move the inches required to reach the remote control.

The weatherman proclaimed it had been the coldest night since 1979. The breakfast news anchors (dressed as if they had been attending a wedding reception) fondled and flirted with each other as if suggested by the producer in their ear. The ugly kind of footsie you have to endure at Beefeater restaurants and office parties.

The pigeons had returned that morning, nesting under the gutter above the living room window, cooing soundly as he had remembered them. He looked to the ceiling and grinned; he had never been happier.

Chapter Twenty-eight

"Nicola"

A bright orange full moon rose in the sky over the roof of the Pillbox, peeking out through drunk clouds. Adam took a long swig from the bottle of Totov in his hand, shutting his eyes because of the pounding sleet, slowly turning to snow in the cold of the night. Heavy vibrations from the music inside crept along through the pavement; six pristine Jaguars sat by the side of the warehouse, their engines purring.

Adam hoisted himself up and around the spiral staircase to the main door on the first floor landing, his heart starting to pound from the Ecstasy he had taken on the train up.

The dance floor was packed considering the weather, and the Pillbox's drainage system – or lack of – which meant rainwater dripped down onto the dance floor from the pipes above. GOMA Kids stood around in small circles, puffing away mindlessly on cigarettes as if they had been smoking for years, they eyes narrowing whenever they inhaled.

Tom, Dick and Harry were on the dance floor to 'Angel of Death' by Slayer, and seemed to be indulging in some new experimental dance motions Tom was trying to teach the other two, who riled Tom with every misstep, with which he would backslap them across the chest and demonstrate how it should be done. The result was scarier than tragic.

Cat was noticeably absent, still sleeping off her excesses at home alone.

Adam pushed through the crowd quickly and purposefully to the back room which was covered with a red curtain, attended to by

Dork, a huge skinhead bouncer, who was also the drummer in a metal band called Chernobyl Super Pussy. Before Adam could ask him if Nicola was there he waved him in without a word.

He pulled the curtain back, revealing a Weimer panorama: Gargoyle figures hung from the wall next to a blacked-out Scottish flag. Below it, Trent sat with some other GOMA Kids at a large wooden table lit by a large candle chandelier. He was grinding his teeth and muttering "d'you have any speed?" at everyone that walked past. He saw Adam and kicked out a seat directly across from him. A large whisky appeared from over Adam's shoulder within seconds.

A boy sitting beside Trent who called himself Nico was kissing a girl that looked about fifteen, brazenly feeling up her insubstantial chest. Trent's eyes wore the redness of a sleepless forty-eight hours, the skin around his nose blotchy and red from excessive coke consumption.

"You know, I really thought you'd have the decency to just stay away from here," he slurred, fingers twitching and shivering. "All things...*considered*."

Adam leaned forward so Trent could hear him above the din, his arms dipping into a puddle of spilled booze on the table. "Where's Nicola? Trent. Where's Nicola?"

He suddenly broke into laughter. "Who's Nicole, what?"

"*Nicola*. I need to speak to her, Trent."

Nico's mouth was chewing air, chanting, "Where's the speed, where's the speed?"

"Shut up, Nico," Trent snapped, punching him once, hard, on the upper arm.

Adam said, "It looks like Mark's been talking to you then."

Trent shrugged. "So."

"So, you're not the only one he's been talking to. He found out me and some GOMA Kids, a wee pillhead called Bug and his bird Fiona were going to crash at the Old Mill, and he sang to the Eton Boys about it. He's why Bug's getting buried tomorrow, and unless they find a way to inflate his body overnight, they'll be burying him in a really long envelope, thanks to Mark and his new crowd."

Trent looked at Nico who was still babbling "where's the speed", only quieter than before.

Adam downed his whisky. "You can ask them, if you like. They're parked downstairs at the side of the building."

"OK, look, what do you want?" Trent asked.

"Just to get out of here in one piece. With Nicola."

He smiled. "She's all yours. If she's still here. Went and dumped me an hour ago. She's been tanking shots at the bar since."

Adam stood up to leave, his bottle of Totov ever present by his side, when he heard Trent pull his chair out too. He paused, his grip on his bottle tightening, ready to swing it on Trent if he needed to, but he was only getting up to find Nico his speed.

Back out on the dancefloor, Fiona was slow-dancing hand in hand with a boy to 'Concubine' by Converge, as bodies went flying around them in the moshpit, tears streaming down her face. *At least she's already wearing black*, Adam thought.

Nicola was standing with her back to him, facing the bar, necking shots as fast the bartender could set them down, a deep crowd still between them, when the side doors were kicked in, the light glimmering off the brass handles of Charles and Edward's canes. A wall of flames swelled from the stairwell they had torched behind them.

The music stopped and the GOMA Kids fled for the exits, all of them blocked by the canes and humourless faces of the Eton Boys.

Nicola was stuck in a crowd surge towards the main doors, her lost eyes catching Adam's who was trying to crawl over the heads of some young rockers in Sonic Youth t-shirts, much to their disgust. "Watch my hair, man," they whined in unison.

"Nicola!" Adam shouted, his arm outstretched, inches away from her fingertips.

Charles climbed up on the bar and started dousing the floor with petrol. He had changed clothes for the occasion, switching his regular suit for a long Victorian overcoat with the collar turned up - like a carriage driver – and, like all the other Eton Boys, had covered his entire face with white paint. Nigel clambered in to the DJ booth and put on Rachmaninov's 3rd Concerto at an ear-splitting volume. Charles cleared his throat over a megaphone, then announced, "This is our music!" The Eton Boys started battering everyone as the hectic piano thrashed overhead.

About thirty more Eton Boys charged in, forcing their way through the crowd, their faces looking stretched, voodoo-like, and they appeared to be chanting 'Long live the union'. They only wanted GOMA Kids, as they didn't stop everyone from leaving. It was easy to tell who they were, anyway; they were the ones in black t-shirts, with badly applied eyeliner. Adam saw a break in the crowd as some GOMA Kids were battered by canes, ducking under the swinging

244

limbs and reaching Nicola, their bodies magnetised to each other. They ducked and weaved their way through the glasses flying through the air and the fire stretching up to the ceiling, letting off a noxious black smoke. Charles directed his Boys around the room from atop the bar, Edward in full flight, sparing no energy. Charles lifted a vodka bottle from off the wall and stuffed a linen handkerchief down the neck, then pulled his silver lighter from his pocket and lit the handkerchief, throwing it into the melee in the middle of the room. Adam pulled the nearest chair up to shield their faces as the bottle exploded, spraying glass all around the room. The Eton Boys doused around the exit door with fuel and lit it, forming a flaming archway. Charles, dancing across the bar on his tiptoes, tipped his hat to Adam and Nicola, belting anyone within range with the brass handle of his cane in perfect synch with the music - he was howling with so much laughter he nearly fell off the bar top.

Adam spotted Fiona running through an unattended fire exit, back where he had come from. Stepping through broken glass that tore through their Converse shoes, they managed to get through the back room to a short corridor leading to two flights of steel grated stairs. At the bottom there was a fire escape door a few inches ajar – and beyond that, moonlight. The stairs were slippery with snow that had been falling since Adam had gone in. He kicked the fire escape door open, which crashed against the wall adjacent. Pigeons flew up everywhere, nearly thirty inside a tiny square, no more than ten by ten feet; four windowless walls rose straight up five or six stories like a wide chimney – the now disused exit at the back of The Pillbox. The pigeons flapped about maniacally about the pair's faces, eventually finding the night sky high above them. The blood from Adam's foot poured out through the sole of his shoe.

"Hold on," he groaned, taking his shoe off to inspect the piece of glass in his foot, yelling out upon its release. His blood leaked smoothly out across the snow, soaking it up, like a red silk veil being pulled across the concrete.

The cold was so intense it felt like pinpricks, but it was calm and silent in the square – the crackle of fire behind them. Smoke spilled silently from a window on the second floor and the screaming was far away on the other side of the building. Some pigeons still pecked around their feet, oblivious to the horror of what was going on. Nicola couldn't move for a second, not sure how to cope with the adrenaline rushing through her body. Adam looked up and felt like he was seeing everything from above; he watched a snowflake slowly falling from a great height, from as high as he could see, slowly frittering down, until it landed on Nicola's cheek, and melted on her skin.

Fiona's tiny footsteps led them down an interminably long alley that joined the car park. Some of the people that had managed to escape were laid out on the ground, but some didn't wait to catch their breath, they just kept on running straight out the main gates, back to the city centre.

The fire had now broken through the roof of the Pillbox and a small crowd gathered at the foot of the metal staircase. There was a long creaking sound – like falling timber – and the roof collapsed through the top floor, flames tickling the moonlight.

The pair leapt in to Nicola's battered VW Beetle, the wheels spinning in the snow. Police cars and fire engines careered into the car park, sirens blaring, and Nicola snatched at the steering wheel to get out their way. The back end of the car skidded away, sending them straight towards a lamppost, only a body-check from another escaping car beside knocking them out of its line.

They sped out of Dalmarnock, running red lights and passing more emergency vehicles on the way. Nicola flitted in and out lane, her hands trembling, with fear and booze. "I don't want to go home, Adam," she sobbed, wiping her eyes every few seconds, only to find them full up again.

Chapter Twenty-nine
'Belmont Memories'

Standing at his living room window, Adam tried to block out all the fucking shouting and screaming and laughing in the distance, and the beer bottles smashing down on the fucking road, next to the tanning salon, blood all over the floor, and a dead pigeon now sitting alone on the warehouse roof. "For God so loved the world!" he started to laugh, then he started to cry. "Some father..."

The living room fire was crackling, the flame still burning blue with cold. Nicola pulled out Adam's tea tray and started rolling a joint, although there was only resin left. It burned quickly and crumbled between her fingers, falling between the tobacco leaves. A gentle warmth rose up from the lighter flame against her face. The joint fizzled satisfactorily as they dragged on it, sensing they were getting the full benefit from the weed. They made balls with their hands and gave each other blowbacks; if for nothing else, it was to feel their breath inside one another, working its way around their lungs, nourishing the weeping waistcoats of their rib cages. Nicola's smoke would circle around Adam's heart – the same as the one she drew on Cat's window – until the blood swelled. They fed each other the last of Adam's Totov vodka – which he had indeed managed to save despite the carnage - and made love, each blissfully in their own high.

When they finished, Nicola put on the woollen jumper lying next to him, the collar bleached white. "This smells of perfume, Adam," she said, sniffing it.

"Yeah, I know. It's yours," he said. "White Light, right?"

"That's right. It's cheap."

249

"Yeah, I know," he laughed.

"*How* do you know?"

"It's a long story." He slipped the joint gently between his lips, his ear drums twitching at the noise of a car engine on the street below. He froze.

"What's wrong?" Nicola asked.

He raised his hand, dropping the joint back in the ashtray. "Do you hear that?" Adam recognised the distinctive splutter.

"So it's a car."

Adam poked the curtain back just far enough to see down to the street with one eye. There, messily screwed into a parking space. "It's my dad's car."

He switched the engine off but didn't get out.

Five years ago to the day, Adam had been rising from bed, ready to get his dad out of his hangover, and to get his mother into the ground.

Nicola leaned forward, taking the opportunity to smoke some more of the joint. "What's he doing?"

"He's just sitting there."

Looking down through the sunroof Adam could only see the top of his head, rocking back and forward, taking hits from a whisky flask. He – like Adam - hadn't been to bed all night. A wreath sat on the passenger seat next to him, that was when Adam realised.

"What date is it today?" he asked, still looking out the window.

"The twenty-first."

Adam sighed, nodding his head once in despondency. "Five years already," he chirped quietly, too quietly for Nicola to hear.

The driver's door opened and he dropped one foot out on to the pavement. Every muscle in Adam's body clenched, unaware if he wanted him to get back in or not. Adam shut his eyes, and after a pause of contemplation, the driver's door shut again and the engine restarted. Adam put his hand up against the window, seeing only the last puff of blue smoke from the exhaust, and for the last time, he never really saw his father.

Adam croaked, "There's somewhere I need to go today."

They stopped at Nicola's house to pick up her things, parking up around the corner in case Nicola's mum asked for Adam to help turn her over again. The car across the road had now been stripped down to its axels.

Nicola was immediately swamped by kids as she opened the door, clinging to her legs as she left. Through the curtains upstairs and downstairs was the glow of TVs: from her mum's bedroom in the dusk light, and in the living room window, where Hugo sat in the single-seater in his tracksuit, anaesthetised as ever, concerned about what he was going to watch now the horse racing was finishing.

"Did you tell your mum you weren't coming back?" Adam asked.

"Yeah," she said, wiping her eyes.

"What did she say to you?"

"'Mind Hugo's prescription.'"

They drove back through the estates one last time, the kids running round the streets playing with litter, the people scrambling to the Poundshops before they closed for the day. And that screaming in

251

earnest. It never ended, and it always sounded the same to Adam. But they wanted someone to hear them. Like someone had lost their way, and they couldn't find their way home again.

Nicola's car barely made it up the Braes to the main gates of the cemetery, swerving all over the place in the snow before coming to a stuttering stop.

"You shouldn't be driving sober," he laughed, handing her the vodka.

She took a long drink, some of it trickling down her neck. "Christ, we might end up dying on the road."

"What a tragedy."

Adam pushed open the rusty iron gates and drove through, the engine spewing out black smoke behind. A groundskeeper watched on from the steps of the bandstand, just to see if he forgot to close the gate - *stupid fucking townie*. Adam gave him a conciliatory wave as they drove past but the man remained expressionless, peering at them.

The tyres struggled to grip down the tree-lined boulevard where one pair of tyre tracks lined the way to the end of the road, the snow shining almost painfully white. Adam looked out the back window at the tracks left behind, then at the pile of their luggage sitting in the back seats.

The same tracks continued up, over the hill, and finished a few feet back from Marie Bernadette's grave. The wreath from his father's car already sat next to the headstone.

Adam laughed, "He'll be back in the pub by now, probably." He got out and placed the flowers in the vase next to the headstone he had tried not to look at for so long. Mairi Bernadette. Beloved wife and mother. 21st December 1992. Adam struggled to repeat his mantra this time, the words sticking in his throat: "It doesn't matter…it was a long time ago."

Third row from the bottom, two rows in.

Nicola held him, bracing him against the wind his dad never saved him from five years before. Thoughts tumbled over from the deepest recesses of his brain; the darkest excesses. From all the hospital visits and painful runs of chemo faded to obscurity and all he could see was the brilliant white landscape. The future.

Through the gaps in the bare trees by the stone cobbled wall, down beyond the edge of the plateau, was Paisley town. Adam thought about his dad sitting at home later that night, like so many lonely drunks with the curtains drawn, as they fell into another stupor. Work for twelve, sleep for eight, and drink for four. Life is all numbers.

At the burned-out newsagents, the traffic lights turned red and a fat woman in a wheelchair rolled past alongside the car.

Adam cracked down the window, exhaling from his cigarette and taking another hit of Totov. "I've seen her before."

She reached down under her tartan blanket and produced a hip flask. Behind her, they were finally taking down the New Labour election poster.

"I wonder how Cat's book is coming along," Nicola said, not really paying attention to anything other than the face on the poster. "What is it called again?"

"Cancer Party," Adam said blankly, passing Nicola the bottle.

"What the hell does that mean?"

Adam stared at the last sheet; at the wide cancer-curing smile and the Eton Boys' tag beside it. Their wonderful father showing them the way forward. And he was leaving like all the other fathers did. "You'd have to ask her," Adam said.

The lights changed but there was still that one sheet left. Nicola touched his leg and the van behind blasted his horn. She hit the accelerator and he knew everything around there was over for him then.

In the rear view mirror the last sheet of Tony's face came down, and just like that, he was gone, erased from Adam's memory, along with the unquestionable mantra, 'Things can only get better'.

Chapter Thirty

'Cancer Party'

The road to the motorway was shut for the relighting of the Paisley Christmas lights Adam had torn down, but a misplaced diversion sign sent them right into the thick of the party.

The main road filled with people swigging openly from bottles and cans. There were more people than could fit on the street, so they scaled the lampposts and hung like monkeys. The police couldn't handle the ever-swelling numbers, so they just stood quietly at the sidelines letting them all get on with it.

There were women on top of their men's shoulders, whooping and shaking their tits about for the crowd. The men cheered and they took off their tops completely and shook them harder (they glowed red from the cold).

The Beetle crawled through the mass of bodies, their flesh pressed against the windows.

Nicola beeped the horn and cursed them under her breath.

Next to them a policeman had slipped into the crowd and was now drinking heavily. He threw his hat away in a moment of drunken exuberance and the man next to him replaced it with a red Santa hat, cuing cheers abound. They embraced each other and shared slugs from a bottle of whisky. Nicola kept blasting the horn but no one noticed. Someone on a stage with a microphone began a mass countdown and the noise reached a crescendo. It was so insanely fevered people were ripping their clothes off, despite the freezing temperatures, and their faces all twisted and tormented like demons as the drink consumed them totally, desperate to see the lights come back on and re-ignite the town.

Adam rolled the windows up as the countdown reached five...
four...three...two...then one. The Christmas lights came on and there
was a hushed silence. A feeling of huge disappointment came over the
crowd. The lights were incredibly dull – as they always had been –
and the electrical reaction of the bulb in the plastic shell of the angel
was enough to tip it over limply from the top of the tree. People started
booing and throwing their bottles towards the compére with the
microphone.

"Is that it?!" someone screamed in abject despair. "This party's
rubbish!"

The lights hung between the shops were as dim as Adam
remembered them. The cheap plastic shells had simply been taped
back together but they didn't hold, breaking open like a Terry's
chocolate orange.

The crowd turned nasty and soon enough the cones lining the
road were hurled into the air like missiles. Punches were thrown and
the car rocked from side to side with the crowd's momentum. The
police cowered in the alleyways unsure what to do; vastly
outnumbered, they hadn't counted on this: a celebration of light going
so terribly wrong. Somehow the message had been lost.

Nicola revved the engine again and changed gear, gently
shunting a few people in front. They turned their anger on the car and
thumped on the bonnet. Luckily they couldn't agree on the best way
to damage the car so, again, they turned on each other and fought
amongst themselves.

Nicola managed to find a clearing in the road just as they started ripping all the decorations back down, tearing them to pieces. The compére appealed for calm but they wouldn't stand for it. They surged towards the stage en masse. A man clambered onstage with his vodka bottle and assumed control by ripping the microphone from the amplifier. He waved everyone else to join him – and they did. The compére was sent flying off the edge of the stage into the crowd, along with the Lord Provost and the other VIP luminaries. The crowd raised their cans and bottles triumphantly.

It was a victory achieved together.

Adam and Nicola were now part of the lights he had seen from his bedroom window, streaming across the motorway flyover, no longer in the distance; they were another one of those lights, seen only in red and white, but from where they were now, they could see the road, they could see the road.

Acknowledgements

I would like to thank my friends for their support and encouragement (in no particular order): Colin, Gerald, Gill, Jo, Tricia, Steph, Ross, Zan.

My colleagues at Waterstone's in Braehead for putting up with my insufferable rants about the state of modern literature and for knowing just when to tell me to shut up, in the nicest way possible.

However, without the punk rock ethos of Mark Buckland at Cargo Publishing you wouldn't be reading this book at all. Since my first public reading he has always been willing to shove me in the face of anyone who would listen.